"Alex, I'm sorry if I embarrassed you," Christian said with a brilliant grin that invited her to grin back.

"That doesn't make it all right," she murmured.

"Will you let me make it up to you over dinner?" he asked.

"No," she said softly, but firmly.

He sighed, as if he was finding wooing her tiring in the extreme. Good, Alex thought, he'll get bored and go away. Why did that fill her with regret?

"I just have to ask why," Christian said, his eyes full of speculation as he leaned closer to her. Alex tried to back away but once more he'd cornered her.

"There's the obvious reason," she said. "Maybe I don't like you."

"That's not what your kiss told me, Alex."

"What did my slap tell you?"

"That you're tempestuous."

"You've got an answer for everything, don't you?"

"No," he murmured. "I haven't a clue who you really are. But I mean to find out." Unable to resist, he bent his head and brushed his lips across hers, again tasting the sweet yearning, the longing to respond, the abrupt retreat of her emotions. He stepped back quickly and caught the hand she lifted to slap him, and kissed her knuckles. "Until we meet again, darling. . . ."

WHAT ARE *LOVESWEPT* ROMANCES?

They are stories of true romance and touching emotion. We believe those two very important ingredients are constants in our highly sensual and very believable stories in the *LOVESWEPT* line. Our goal is to give you, the reader, stories of consistently high quality that may sometimes make you laugh, sometimes make you cry, but are always fresh and creative and contain many delightful surprises within their pages.

Most romance fans read an enormous number of books. Those they truly love, they keep. Others may be traded with friends and soon forgotten. We hope that each *LOVESWEPT* romance will be a treasure—a "keeper." We will always try to publish

LOVE STORIES YOU'LL NEVER FORGET
BY AUTHORS YOU'LL ALWAYS REMEMBER

The Editors

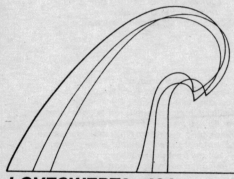

LOVESWEPT® • 434

Tami Hoag
Tempestuous

 BANTAM BOOKS
NEW YORK • TORONTO • LONDON • SYDNEY • AUCKLAND

TEMPESTUOUS

A Bantam Book / November 1990

*LOVESWEPT® and the wave device are registered
trademarks of Bantam Books, a division of
Bantam Doubleday Dell Publishing Group, Inc.
Registered in U.S. Patent
and Trademark Office and elsewhere.*

*If you would be interested in receiving protective vinyl
covers for your Loveswept books, please write to this
address for information:*

> Loveswept
> Bantam Books
> P. O. Box 985
> Hicksville, NY 11802

ISBN 0-553-44065-9

Published simultaneously in the United States and Canada

PRINTED IN THE UNITED STATES OF AMERICA

OPM   0 9 8 7 6 5 4 3 2 1

One

"Good Lord, she's lovely!" Christian Atherton murmured, his accent carrying the undiluted, polished tones of a British public-school student. As he came to attention his shoulders pulled back beneath the fine wool of his navy jacket. His square chin came up a notch above his neatly knotted maroon tie, emphasizing the classic lines of his lean face. In response to the tensing of his muscles his horse shifted restively beneath him.

His attention was locked on the young woman riding into the show ring to collect a blue ribbon. He'd been a connoisseur of women for nearly twenty-two years, ever since the summer he'd turned thirteen and the gardener's daughter had suddenly developed breasts. The lady he had his eye on now was well worth a long look.

"Who is she?"

"Where have you been? Living in a cave?" drawled Robert Braddock, his voice as rich and Southern as pecan pie. His wide mouth cut upward in a sharp, handsome smile. He leaned lazily against the pommel of his saddle, showing none of the form that had made him one of the top hunter-jumper trainers in Virginia at the tender age of twenty-seven.

"Close," Christian said dryly. "I've just spent three weeks in England at the family mausoleum, better known as Westerleigh Manor. Uncle Richard passed away."

Braddock's manners asserted themselves, and he

straightened in his saddle out of respect for the dead. "I'm sorry, Chris."

"Don't be." Christian grinned at his friend and rival, a brilliant square white smile that made him look exactly what he was—handsome, aristocratic, and a bit of a rake. "Uncle Dicky was ninety-seven. He drank like a fish, drove like a maniac, and died—er—in the saddle, so to speak. He had a wonderful life and a pleasant passing. We should all be so lucky."

His neon-blue eyes took on a slightly wistful expression, and the glittering good humor that usually resided there faded momentarily as he sighed. Uncle Dicky was dead. The stuffy Athertons were down to one black sheep—him.

"Alexandra Gianni," Braddock said, answering Christian's original question. "Cold as a pump handle on a January morning," he added in ill-disguised disgust.

"Turned you down, did she?" Christian said dryly, arching a brow.

"She's been here three weeks and has managed to say one word to every fella who's asked her out—no."

"Well, that just shows she has good taste and sound judgment."

"I suppose you think you can do better?"

"Please," Christian drawled disdainfully. "Of course I could do better. Admit it, Braddock, you've won your share of dim-witted stable girls, but you're simply not in my league."

"You pompous ass," Braddock said with a good-natured grin. "I'll bet you don't get anywhere with her either. You might be the Casanova of the show-jumping world, but this lady would give the iceberg that sank the Titanic a run for its money."

Christian's speculative gaze settled again on Alexandra Gianni. She didn't look the ice-maiden type to him. With her olive complexion and dark eyes, her unruly short black hair and lush mouth, she looked more like the hot, feisty type. Tempestuous.

The type to stand toe-to-toe with a man in a fight and rake her nails down his back in bed.

Braddock turned and grinned at him suddenly. "How much do you want to bet?"

"I beg your pardon?"

"Put your money where your mouth is, Romeo," he challenged. "I'll bet you a hundred dollars you can't get her to go with you to Hayden Hill's big bash before the Green Hills Jumper Classic."

Christian barked a laugh of surprise that startled his horse. The thoroughbred danced beneath him, and he quieted the gelding with a hand on the horse's neck, never taking his eyes off Braddock. "That's more than a month away! Have you developed a sudden yearning for poverty?"

"You forget, my friend," Braddock said slyly. "I've spoken with the lady. I have firsthand experience and the frostbite to prove it. A hundred says she won't go with you."

Christian considered the outrageous wager for a moment. It appealed to the reckless rogue in him, the quality that made his stiff-necked family shake their heads in disappointment. He thought of what Uncle Dicky would have done, and grinned. "Make it a thousand and it's a deal."

Braddock's dark eyes glowed with delight and greed. "You've got yourself a bet, my friend."

Two

"Good job, honey," Tully Haskell said in parting.

Alex murmured a thank-you and turned toward the stalls she had rented for the day. She jumped and gasped when the man patted her fanny, but when she wheeled to glare at him, he was calmly walking away as if what he'd done hadn't been the least bit out of line.

Alex stood in the aisle, fuming for a moment, then turned to stare pensively at the stalls of her two star performers, both owned by Haskell. A Touch of Dutch, the sweet-tempered mare she'd just won on, and Terminator, an arrogant, ill-mannered lout—not unlike his owner. That was the world in a nutshell. Females were meek and malleable, and males took what they wanted.

Everything inside Alex tightened against the memory that tried to surface. Squeezing her eyes shut, she fought it with every scrap of willpower she had, succeeding only in fighting back the images themselves, not the feelings they evoked. Her muscles tensed until she was trembling.

When a large male hand settled on her shoulder, she didn't think, didn't question, didn't turn to confront. She simply reacted as she had been trained to react. A second later Christian Atherton lay sprawled on the cobbled floor at her feet.

Alex stared, wide-eyed, aghast at what she'd just done. She had just heaved the three-time American Grand Prix Association Rider of the Year over her shoulder. She had just slammed to the floor one of the most highly regarded people in her profession.

"Oh, no . . ." Her groan mingled with his. She slapped a hand to her forehead and cursed herself in rapid Italian.

Christian sat up gingerly, wincing at the stinging pain in his shoulders and back. He'd been thrown from horses with less force. Shaking his head to clear it, he looked up at Alexandra Gianni with a stunned expression. Petite, dainty Alexandra Gianni, who stood no more than five feet five.

"I say, are you a former commando or something?"

"I'm sorry," Alex whispered, too mortified to speak any louder. She bit her lip and squeezed her eyes shut again, wishing the scene would disappear by the time she opened them.

This was no way to build a favorable reputation in Virginia, she scolded herself. Flinging influential people around was not going to win her friends or respect. She had learned to live without the first, but the second was essential.

She put a hand over her eyes and peeked cautiously through her fingers. Christian was still sitting on the stable floor. He had taken up a relaxed pose, with one knee drawn up and an arm draped across it. He stared down the corridor at the half-dozen people staring back at him, a look of annoyance drawing his brows together and twisting his handsome mouth. His champagne blond hair fell rakishly across his forehead. All in all, he looked damned sexy.

Alex imagined he looked that way regardless. Her heart was pounding, and she knew it had little to do with the exertion of throwing him over her shoulder. She could have told herself it was because he had startled her. She could have told herself it had nothing to do with the fact that Christian Atherton was even better looking in person than he was on the glossy pages of the horse magazines. She could have told herself those things, but they would have been lies.

"I'm really so sorry," she mumbled in an agony of embarrassment.

"So you said. Do you always go about throwing chaps to the ground, or was I singled out?" he questioned, his cultured tone martini dry.

"You snuck up on me!" Alex said accusingly, tossing her hands up, then grabbing them back against her as if she were trying to recapture and subdue her emotional outburst. She looked more guilty for having openly reacted than for hurling Christian to the cobblestones. Taking a calming breath, she composed herself and said, "You shouldn't have snuck up on me."

"I see." Christian's brows rose and fell. There was a whole passel of odd mysteries to decipher just in her action and reaction. He shook his head again. "Well, I've always known better than to approach a horse from behind. I guess I should add women to that rule of thumb as well."

"I'm really very sorry," Alex said, contrite again, holding out a hand to help him up.

Christian eyed her hand dubiously. "I'm not sure I should accept that," he said dryly. "Do you promise not to twist my arm behind my back and slam me face first into a post?"

Alex couldn't help but laugh in both relief and humor. He was taking it better than most men would have. She had humiliated him in front of his peers, and he was looking up at her with twinkling blue eyes and a wry, self-deprecating smile.

Her own smile faded as she realized how easily he had breached her mental defenses with that infamous grin of his. Professionally, he would be a very good man to befriend. Personally, he would be a very dangerous man for her to be around.

"I'll be on my best behavior," she promised soberly.

"That may not be saying very much," Christian teased, taking hold of her small hand. "But I guess I'll have to trust you."

He rose gracefully to his feet, somehow managing

not to look rumpled in the least. Not even his maroon necktie was out of place, Alex marveled as she gazed up at him, unable to keep from admiring his appearance.

He wasn't overly tall, perhaps an inch or so shy of six feet, but his physique was athletic and elegant. His shoulders filled his custom-tailored coat to perfection. His hips were narrow, his thighs the thighs of dancers and horsemen—powerful with long, solid muscles that were blatantly displayed by the tight knit of his expensive buff breeches. The black boots that rose to his knees were impeccably polished.

While Alex looked him over, Christian returned the favor, though his perusal was much slower, much more openly appreciative than her surreptitious glances. His gaze poured down over her with all the slow heat of sun-warmed honey, taking in her petite frame as if she were much taller, infinitely more voluptuous, and clad in something far sexier than riding togs.

Alex almost looked down to make certain her jacket and breeches hadn't somehow been miraculously transformed into a diaphanous negligee. She felt stripped naked by his blue eyes, and as a flush spread under her skin, she hooked a finger beneath the choker of her blouse and tugged at it in an attempt to breathe easier.

Christian smiled to himself, well aware of her reaction to his slow assessment of her, and well aware of his own body's response. He liked what he saw.

Her hair shone blue black under the soft light of the stable. It was cut severely short on the sides and in back, but was longer on top, thick and wild with a tendency to spill across her forehead. The boyishness of the cut did nothing to detract from the almost pixielike femininity of her features. In fact, the simplicity of the style drew the eye to appreciate the delicate lines of her oval face—the high, well-defined cheekbones, the slim straight nose, the lush pouty mouth. Christian groaned inwardly, desire stirring deep in his belly. Very kissable, that mouth.

Continuing on with the visual tour he realized there was a slightly defiant tilt to her chin. Sassy. And her eyes were not the dark brown he had thought them to be, but a dark translucent shade of amber set with flecks of gold: Beautiful, intense, and . . . what? . . . wary? How odd.

Alex shifted uncomfortably and tried to extricate her hand from his grasp. He held it firmly but gently. There was nothing punishing or aggressive in his grasp. He merely let her know with a slight tightening of his fingers that he wasn't quite ready to let go of her. No wonder his horses were so good, she thought. With hands like his there would be no fighting the bit; he would simply guide, quietly insist, and get his way every time—just as he was getting his way now.

"Let's pretend you didn't try to permanently disable me, and we'll begin this conversation again," he suggested, his dazzling smile still in place.

"I suppose I can't pass up an offer like that," Alex said, doing her best to ignore the warm sliding sensation in her stomach. She couldn't afford to let Christian Atherton affect her in that way. They were simply fellow professional riders. The fact that he was charmingly, deliciously male, and she was susceptibly female, couldn't enter into it.

Christian resisted the urge to grind his teeth at her less-than-enthusiastic reply. She didn't have to sound so bloody resigned about it. Didn't she realize there were plenty of women who would have fought her tooth and nail for the chance to hold his hand? And she would likely knock them all flat, he thought, unable to suppress his amusement.

"Christian Atherton," he said, giving her a smile.

Television didn't do him justice, Alex thought. On television Christian Atherton was merely handsome. In person, he was dazzling. He had the air of a prince—self-assured, confident of his own brilliant qualities and the responses those qualities would elicit from the mere mortals around him.

It almost made Alex laugh to think he had introduced himself. As if there weren't a girl or woman interested in horses who didn't know him on sight! Christian Atherton was the golden boy of the show-jumping world. His career accomplishments included wins at every major show in America and abroad. He also had a notorious reputation for being a playboy. By all accounts he had garnered as many feminine hearts as he had blue ribbons over the years. It wasn't difficult to imagine why.

No, Alex thought wryly, it wasn't difficult to imagine why this man had women falling at his booted feet. The difficult thing was keeping her own feminine reaction to his aristocratic looks to herself. Fortunately—or unfortunately—she had had plenty of practice at hiding her emotions over the past couple of years. Her expression remained carefully blank, giving away none of her inner turmoil.

"I'm Alex Gianni. What can I do for you, Mr. Atherton?" Alex asked neutrally. This time when she pulled back her hand, he let her go.

"Call me Christian, for starters," he said smoothly. "I'm afraid I had the frightfully bad manners to be abroad when you moved into the neighborhood. I haven't had a chance to welcome you to Briarwood, Ms. Gianni. I insist on making it up to you. What do you say to lunch tomorrow and a little motor tour of the area?"

Oh, no, Alex thought, groaning inwardly as her heart jumped and sank. Another one. What was it about her that attracted so much male attention? She really couldn't figure it out. She didn't think herself particularly beautiful. She didn't have the kind of figure to turn male heads. She wasn't the least bit flirtatious or even encouraging. She had, in fact, done everything she could think of to *avoid* attracting attention of any kind. Still, in the three weeks since she and her baby daughter Isabella had settled on the little farm outside of Briarwood, she'd had no less than a half-dozen offers for dates.

And now Christian Atherton, the man whose poster adorned the bedrooms of every horse-crazy girl in the Western world, had set his sights on her. It was too ironic. At some point in her past she would have been flattered at having him merely speak to her, let alone ask her out. She would have been bubbling over with excitement. But those days were past. Now she was simply rattled and vaguely disappointed.

"I'm sorry, Mr. Atherton," she said with deceptive calm. "I'm afraid I don't have much time for that kind of thing. Thank you for offering, though."

"Come now," Christian insisted. "We should get to know each other, don't you think?"

The glow in his laser blue eyes made his suggestion seem much more intimate than neighborly. He stood half a step closer than was strictly necessary—close enough to make Alex uncomfortably aware of him, and yet not so close that she had a good excuse to move away. The man was a master and he knew it. The teasing lights in his eyes told Alex he knew exactly what he was doing to her and that he knew she knew. It was all a marvelous game to him, charming women into joining the ranks of his conquests. Everyone was aware up front what the rules and the stakes were—fun, nothing serious; no harm, no foul.

Alex felt herself relaxing and realized it was dangerous. Christian Atherton may not have been threatening, but he was a threat—one she had to nip in the bud. She acknowledged the truth with a frighteningly strong sense of regret. It might have been fun. . . .

"I know all about you," she said, a wry smile lifting one corner of her wide mouth.

"My reputation has preceded me?" He quirked a brow and looked immensely pleased with himself. It was an expression that changed quickly to a comical scowl when she answered.

"Sure. My mother warned me about men like you when I turned thirteen."

"Surely you didn't listen," Christian chided, his eyes sparkling with good humor.

No, Alex thought, glancing away, her own teasing expression melting into sudden pensiveness, she hadn't listened. Maybe if she had listened, she would still have been married, would still have been in California, would still have the unqualified, untried support of her family. But she hadn't listened, and now all of those things were lost to her.

"I prefer the smile," Christian murmured gently, leaning closer. He didn't know where she'd gone in those few seconds, but it wasn't a happy place. She looked haunted and regretful, and he felt a strong desire to put his arms around her in a show of comfort, but he doubted she would have appreciated the gesture. Instead, he reached out and brushed her wild black curls back from her forehead, leaning closer so that when he spoke his voice was just above a whisper, smooth and velvety. "The gold flecks in your eyes light up when you smile."

For a moment Alex merely stared at him, mesmerized by his gaze, his voice, the gentle concern in his eyes. It felt strange to be so close to him, to be enveloped by the awesome power of his personality. In a way it felt as intimate as anything she had ever encountered, and yet they weren't even touching. It was intoxicating . . . and dangerous.

Finally she shook herself out of her brooding reverie and looked up at him, suddenly all business, self-preservation uppermost in her mind. "I might as well tell you straight out to save your charm, Mr. Atherton. It's wasted on me."

"Charm is never wasted on a beautiful woman," Christian argued, lifting his chin up a notch. He planted one hand on the stall door beside her and leaned a millimeter closer.

He'd played this hard-to-get-game before. It required determination, but it was always worth the extra effort. There was fire beneath Alexandra Gianni's ice.

He could see it in her amber eyes, in the stubborn set of her chin, in the line of that lush, lush mouth. He wanted to be the one to melt the ice and bring that fire out. He wanted to be the one to feel those flames lick over him and consume him.

It had nothing to do with the wager. He didn't need the money, nor did his ego need the boost. It had to do with challenge. It had to do with feelings that dated back to the first man and woman, feelings that were a little more primitive than what he was used to feeling. They intrigued him. Alex intrigued him.

"Thank you for the compliment," Alex murmured, pressing back against the post between her stalls in an unconscious effort to escape not only the man but the force of his personality as well.

Her resolve wavered as she took in the frankly appreciative look Christian was giving her. That warm sliding sensation stirred her insides again as her own gaze settled on his mouth. It was wide and mobile with firm, well-cut lips and a seemingly endless repertoire of sexy smiles.

She couldn't help but wonder what it would be like to have him kiss her. The thought was unwanted, unwelcome, but it managed to get past her considerable will just the same. It had been so long since she'd had a man kiss her with the kind of tenderness and passion she instinctively knew this one was capable of. She'd been so alone for so long. . . .

He read the message in her eyes unerringly and lowered his head a fraction of an inch in invitation, his lips hovering just a breath above hers. But before she could take him up on his offer, her defenses reasserted themselves and she ducked away, kneeling to dig her gloves out of her gear bag.

What was the matter with her, she wondered angrily. Her hands were shaking as she fussed unnecessarily with the big red duffel bag that held all her personal paraphernalia. She knew exactly what Christian Atherton was. He was a rake and a womanizer, and she didn't have the time or the desire to play his kind of game. Nor would he want to play with her once they had gotten to know each other. Lord knew he would probably set a new sprint record getting away from her once he discovered who she really was.

"Merely stating fact," Christian drawled, leaning lazily against the narrow post. "If a woman is beautiful, she deserves to be told."

"And if she's not?"

He grinned. "Then I tell her anyway."

He was by nature a flatterer. It was a skill he had perfected as a child. Even at the tender age of four he had known the fairer sex enjoyed praise. He'd filled his piggy bank time and again with the quarters his aunts and his mother's friends had rewarded him with for his astute observations.

In Alex's case it was entirely justified. She was very lovely in a sophisticated way. The longer he looked at her, the more he liked what he saw. Hers was a beauty that was at once subtle and exotic, and he realized with a start that she wasn't wearing a scrap of makeup, not even mascara, nothing to emphasize or draw the eye. He also realized that she wasn't entirely comfortable with his compliment or his scrutiny. He got the distinct impression she would rather he had not noticed her at all.

He watched with a mixture of confusion and amusement as she busied herself taking items out of her bag and putting them back in. She was rattled, and she clearly didn't like being rattled. Information worth filing away for future reference, he noted.

"You're extremely tidy," he said pleasantly, bending over to peer into her gear bag. When he turned his head toward her, he was again within kissing distance. He smiled lazily. "A quality nearly as priceless as your looks."

Alex flushed, suddenly hot beneath her proper white cotton blouse and charcoal jacket. "Care to look at my teeth while you're at it?" she asked dryly.

"I have," he admitted. "They're adorable. I like the way the front two on top overlap slightly. Gives you a certain innocent quality."

"Complimenting women is a hobby of yours." She said it as if he would be put off by her knowing that about him.

Christian chuckled. "More like a calling, actually."

"You do it very well," Alex said, the corners of her mouth cutting upwards as that dangerous relaxation stole through her again. She couldn't seem to resist the urge to like him. His irreverently charming manner made it difficult to think he could ever be a danger to her.

"Thank you," he said, straightening only to lean indolently against a stall door once again, as if he found it necessary to reserve his strength for more important things than standing around.

"But you're wasting your time on me if you think anything will come of it," Alex warned, struggling once more to resurrect her cool reserve. She pushed herself to her feet and tugged on her thin black leather gloves. "I've got a stable to run and a daughter to raise. I'm afraid my schedule doesn't allow for flirtations."

His brows lifted in a show of mock surprise and shock. "Doesn't allow?" He shook his head and sighed dramatically. "My dear girl, flirtations are an essential part of life—like good horses and really fine wine."

Alex looked up at him, frustrated. She was trying to be serious, trying to set things straight between them right off. She couldn't afford another misunderstanding; the last one had cost her too much. She didn't want there to be any question in Christian Atherton's mind about her intentions. And he had the gall to stand there and tease her, looking impossibly handsome and terribly British and damned sexy.

He shot her an infectious, lopsided grin that easily cracked all her barriers as if they had been constructed of eggshells. She shook her head in amazement and managed a weary laugh. "You don't give up easily, do you?"

"I never give up," Christian declared, the unmistakable steely glint of determination brightening his eyes and threading through his smooth, pleasant voice. "I am on rare occasions beaten, but I *never* give up."

"You're doomed to defeat this time. I feel it only fair to warn you."

He clearly didn't believe her. Of course, she couldn't have expected him to. Men like Christian Atherton had a boundless belief in their own appeal to women. Most of them came across as arrogant. This one came across as endearing. Alex would have preferred the arrogance; it was much easier to resist.

"We'll see," he said absently. "You have a daughter. Can I assume you're divorced? I'd hate to discover I've set my sights on a married lady. That is my one absolutely unbreakable rule—no married ladies."

"It's nice to know you have at least one scruple," Alex reflected dryly. "Yes, I'm divorced."

There didn't seem to be any harm in revealing that much about her background. The alternative—letting people believe Isabella had been born out of wedlock—went too strongly against her grain. Her daughter had in fact been born after her divorce from Michael DeGrazia, but she had been conceived in love, regardless of what Michael chose to think. It wasn't Isabella's fault her parents' marriage hadn't been able to withstand the pressure inflicted on it by forces both from the outside and from within.

"Recently divorced?"

She gave Christian an apologetic look and moved to the door of Terminator's stall. "I'd love to stand around here and play *This is Your Life,* but I have a competition to get ready for."

"After then? Over dinner?" he said with another of his smiles. "There's an excellent Italian restaurant in Briarwood. The owner is a friend of mine."

"Then maybe she'll eat with you," Alex suggested

sweetly. "I have chores to do and a baby to take care of."

"All right," Christian said on a good-humored sigh. He bowed slightly. "I concede round one to you, Ms. Gianni. What competition are you getting ready for?"

"Open jumper."

She swung the stall door open and let Christian get his first good look at her mount. His eyes widened in horror.

"Oh my Lord, it can't be," he muttered, staring. But there was no mistaking the big, rawboned, washy chestnut gelding with the distinctive crooked white stripe running down his face. "I thought they'd shot him."

"Not yet," Alex said through her teeth. It was one thing for her to think nasty things of the horses she trained—and she had plenty about this one—but having a fellow trainer express those same thoughts aloud was another thing altogether. It rankled.

Christian turned away from the horse and gave her an incredulous look as a riot of unfamiliar feelings tore loose inside him. There was a strangely urgent note in his voice when he said, "You can't be serious about riding this beast."

"It's what I get paid to do," she said stiffly, shoving her helmet down on her head and buckling the chin strap.

"There isn't enough money in the commonwealth of Virginia to make it worth your while."

Your opinion, Alex thought darkly. It would be easy for him to refuse horses like Terminator. Quaid Farm, the stable Christian rode for, had paddocks full of top-quality, beautifully bred, beautifully behaved animals. Christian also reportedly had enough money of his own to make riding strictly a hobby. She, on the other hand, had to charge bargain rates, beg for mounts, and be grateful even for evil-tempered jugheads like Terminator.

"I'm serious, Alex," Christian said, and indeed he was. The corners of his handsome mouth were turning down. A line of disapproval etched itself between his eyebrows. He looked as serious as a banker. "I've never had the misfortune of riding Terminator myself, but I am well aware of the horse's reputation. It actually frightens me to think of you climbing up on that animal's back. You can't weigh much more than seven stone, and you don't look particularly strong. That beast is as big as a freight train with a mouth like granite and a disturbed, diabolical mind."

As if to illustrate the point Terminator struck out at him with a front foot as he was led from the stall, and Christian had to jump back out of the way or lose a kneecap. Eyes flashing, ears pinned, the gelding danced restlessly in the aisle while Alex snugged up the girth on her saddle.

"You're new around here," Christian said, planting his hands on his slim hips. "That's the only way anyone ever gets on this brute. I saw him in a point-to-point race at Oatlands before he began his show career. He went berserk at the ninth fence and ran himself into a tree. Pity he wasn't killed," he muttered, shaking his head. "That was when it was decided that he would be better off confined to jumping in an arena." He eyed the gelding with open dislike. "He's changed hands more times than a bad used car. Who owns him now?"

"Tully Haskell."

"Bloody hell."

It was on the tip of his tongue to give Alex his undiluted opinion of the man she was riding for, but she had her hands full trying to get Terminator out of the barn without incident. Muttering under his breath about men who take advantage of innocent women, Christian nudged Alex aside, took the recalcitrant animal by the bridle, and coerced him out into the bright April sunshine.

Alex slapped her crop against her boot and fumed, her ready temper rising to the surface. Who did he think he was, telling her what horses she should or should not ride, what owners she should or should not do business with? Who did he think he was, charming her off her feet one minute, then belittling her judgment and her ability the next?

"I'll take my horse now, Mr. Atherton," she said, deftly avoiding Terminator's teeth as she reached for his reins.

Christian refused to let go of the horse's head. He gave Alex a grave look that would have done his stuffier relatives proud. "If you have any sense, you'll send both this rogue and his owner packing. They're nothing but trouble, the pair of them."

"Thank you for sharing your opinion with me," she said with a sneer. Leaving the reins to him, she went to the horse's side and vaulted quickly into the saddle. Terminator danced, shaking his head violently against Christian's hold. Alex gathered up the reins and settled her feet firmly in the irons. She looked down at Christian with golden fire snapping in her eyes. "I don't have the luxury of picking and choosing my clients, Mr. Atherton. This horse can jump, and I can ride him. It's not always fun, but it's what I get paid to do, and since I don't have a family fortune to fall back on, I do it without complaint."

Christian winced at the dressing-down. He'd obviously struck a nerve. Dammit, it wasn't like him to go spouting off that way, telling other people what to do. His brothers had made careers of it, but he had always adhered to a strict laissez-faire policy. It was none of his business what other people did with their lives. Why he had suddenly deviated from that philosophy, he didn't know. It was clear, however, that Alex hadn't appreciated it.

"Alex, I'm sorry," he started.

"Tell someone who cares," she said, her concentration on her horse. Terminator's muscles were bunched and trembling beneath her. It was like sitting on a volcano that was ready to blow. Already there were dark stains of sweat on his neck and foam edging his mouth.

She shot Christian a glance, the genuine apology

and concern in his eyes going straight to her heart. She gave him a lopsided smile. "You can wish me luck."

"Yes." He nodded, letting go of the bridle and waving her off.

The big gelding bounded away, struggling furiously for control of the bit for five strides before giving in and settling into a strong, ground-eating canter.

Christian sighed and shifted his weight from foot to foot, physically uncomfortable with his sudden overwhelming concern for another person. He thought of himself as the consummate bachelor, concerned with only his own needs, responsible for no one but himself. That was the way he had lived his entire life.

As the fourth son of the Earl of Westly, he was far down the line when it came to looking after the family business. His stiff-necked older brothers had taken up those reins of responsibility, leaving him to take up reins of another kind.

He had signed on as trainer at Quaid Farm because he hadn't wanted the responsibility of running his own place. He had remained single because he had never wanted the responsibility of a wife. And now he stood watching Alexandra Gianni fighting with that devil of a horse, feeling responsible because he hadn't convinced her to stay off the ruddy beast!

Gads. What would Uncle Dicky have said?

"Losing your touch, your lordship?" a sardonic voice drawled from beside him.

Christian dragged his attention away from Alex, who had taken Terminator across the field to work off his initial burst of hatefulness, and turned toward the source of the amused drawl. Robert Braddock stood beside him, idly paging through the catalog of a pricey tack shop. Braddock was just his equal in height, but stockier and swarthy. In another era he could have been a pirate or a Gypsy. The beginnings of laughter twitched the corners of his lips and sent lines fanning out beside his dark eyes.

"What do you want?" Christian asked irritably. He had no doubt Robert had ferreted out every detail of the undignified greeting he'd received from Alex in the alleyway of the stable. It wouldn't have surprised him had Braddock somehow managed to produce a videotape of his humiliation. Robert took great pride in being the first on the show circuit to know everything about anything that was going on. It was a trait Christian had always found irksome; he generally considered gossip beneath his dignity. He narrowed his eyes now and tried to think of the most conspicuous, frivolous, insulting way he could spend his friend's money once he won the bet.

"What's this? Bad manners from my British buddy?" Robert teased mercilessly, his dark eyes dancing. "My, my, what would the queen say?"

"She'd say you were an obnoxious pig. Do go away."

"Ah, well, I've got better things to think about, like how I'm gonna spend my thousand bucks. Think I'll start with a new pair of custom-made boots."

"I'll feed you the ones you're wearing in a minute," Christian said, his ego smarting just a little too much to have his pal pour salt on the wound.

"Tsk, tsk, Christian," Braddock said, shaking his head. "Your frostbite is showing."

"Shove off."

Robert sighed happily and turned a page in his catalog. "I'm just thinking I might buy myself a new jacket to go with the boots. Think I'd look good in pinstripes?"

Christian raised a disdainful brow. "Considering where you normally shop, I should think you could replace your entire wardrobe twice over for a thousand dollars, but that's irrelevant. You shan't have the money."

"Oh, really? I think that little tumble you took over Ms. Gianni's shoulder rattled your brains, friend. Too bad you weren't wearing your helmet. There're some good ones in this catalog." he said slyly, fanning the pages in Christian's face. "Maybe I'll be nice and buy you one with your own money."

Christian gave him a long, cool look, then smiled like a crocodile. "I am going to take great delight in humiliating you with your cash, Robert. I wonder what billboards cost these days."

"You'll never need to know." Braddock folded the catalog and tucked it beneath one arm. "Just to make things clear up front—you do realize this has to be an honest-to-gosh date you get with her. You have to escort her to the party, eat with her, dance with her, and kiss her in full view of everybody."

"Really, Robert," Christian said with distaste, "you can be absolutely adolescent."

"Those are the terms," Braddock said, unruffled. "Agreed?"

Christian rolled his eyes. "Agreed."

He could, after all, be just as adolescent as the next man. There was no reason for him not to be. He had no one to answer to. There was no harm in a little wager between gentlemen. It wasn't as if the lady in question would be hurt in any way. They would both enjoy a nice night out, Christian would be a thousand dollars richer, and Robert would be a poorer but wiser man. It seemed a good deal all around.

They turned their attention to Alex and Terminator as she worked him in circles in their own private corner of the field, staying well away from the other horses and riders.

"What do you know about her?" Christian asked.

"Not much more than I already told you. She's renting that place down the hill from you, taking on horses to train and show. Got some girls taking lessons from her. But as far as where she came from and how she got here—that's a mystery."

"Hmmm . . ." Christian mused, his curiosity more than piqued by Alex Gianni. "I do love a good mystery."

"Well, pal, you'd better hit the bookstore then and

stock up, because that little lady isn't interested in playing Sherlock and Dr. Watson with anybody."

"We'll see."

"Look at the way she sits that old boy," Braddock said in admiration. "Deep in the saddle, solid as a rock. She's good."

"Yes, quite," Christian agreed. "Too good to be getting herself killed on the likes of that ill-bred nag. Tully Haskell has sunk to a new low, foisting Terminator off on an unsuspecting young woman. If she gets hurt . . ." The threat trailed off as he realized what he was saying.

A shudder snaked through his lean body. Where had this sudden virtuous streak come from? It wasn't any of his business what went on between Alex Gianni and Tully Haskell. It certainly wasn't his place to act as either guardian or avenging angel. Good Lord, he wasn't now, nor did he ever want to be, responsible for Alex Gianni or anyone else!

"You all right?" Robert asked, concerned. "You're looking a might pale."

"I'm fine," Christian muttered. "Just the leftover bits of something I picked up in England."

"Speaking of things you picked up in England," Braddock drawled sardonically as his gaze homed in on the slim young woman striding toward them in fashionably tattered jeans and a black-leather motorcycle jacket.

Christian groaned from the bottom of his heart.

"Blimey, gov, I heard you flipped for some bird in the stables!" the woman exclaimed, her cockney accent ringing out as loudly as the bells of Saint Mary's Church. She stopped several feet away from them, doubling over as she dissolved into a fit of laughter. "Flipped! Crikey, I'd 'a' killed to see that! His nibs sprawled out on the cobblestones, tossed over by a lady!"

"Charlotte, must you always use a tone of voice loud enough to drown out aircraft engines?" Christian hissed between his teeth.

The girl's outburst had drawn amused stares from

all around them. Snickers went through the little knots of people like ripples moving outward from one loud splash in a pond. There was no hope of keeping the little incident with Alex a secret, of course, but he would have preferred to have had the gossip spread by someone other than one of his own grooms.

She laughed, waving a hand at him. "Oh, Go on! Ain't nobody here what hasn't heard the tale half a dozen times already!" she exclaimed, dropping all the *H*s off her words in typical East End fashion.

Braddock rubbed a hand across his jaw to discreetly cover his grin. Christian turned a dull red and spoke through clenched teeth. "Charlotte, you are the bane of my existence."

"Oh, go on!" She laughed and batted his arm, not contrite in the least.

Charlotte "Charlie" Simmonds was eighteen, a petite cockney firecracker with an accent as thick as London fog, and burgundy hair, which she wore combed straight up. It was shorn off on the top and looked as thick and flat as the yew hedges in Windsor Great Park. Christian suspected she got it to stay up that way through sheer stubbornness. Her face was still slightly round with baby fat and striking due to an overabundance of eye makeup and dark lipstick. A cluster of earrings dangled from her right lobe. The left one held a single garnet stud.

She was the niece of Old Ned, head stable lad at Westerleigh Manor. "A bright, precocious girl," Ned had called her. "Needs to see a bit o' the world, is all," he'd said. "Her dad run off and her mum drinks a bit, and there's no proper jobs about for a girl her age."

There had been a kind of desperation in his eyes at the time, and Christian could only wonder now why he hadn't taken heed of the signs. Ned had fairly begged him to take the girl back to Virginia with him. He had yet to figure out why he had said yes.

"You might be slipping, luv," Charlie said, digging

him in the ribs with her bony elbow. "The ladies are supposed to fall at your feet, not the other way round!"

Christian bit back half a dozen different remarks, all along the lines of "mind your betters." He cursed a royal blue streak under his breath. Each and every one of those remarks were things his brothers might have said to the servants. One couldn't say those sorts of things in America. According to ideology no one had any "betters" here. It was one of the reasons he had moved to the States—to get away from the blue blooded, stuffy class system he'd grown up in. And here he was, ready to revert to type at a little needling from an impudent teenager. Maybe he *was* slipping.

"What's the matter, ducky?" Charlie asked, squinting so that her eyes became tiny bright spots of brown in her pixie face. "Can't take a little ribbing? Stuffy, stuffy," she scolded in a singsong voice, shaking a finger at him.

"Oh, don't be so tedious," Christian grumbled, scowling at her. "I ought to give you the sack for lack of proper respect."

He grimaced the instant the words were out of his mouth. Uncle Dicky would have been rolling in his grave if they hadn't cremated him and scattered him over Cheltenham racecourse.

"Right. Right. Go on. Go ahead and fire me," Charlie said lightly, shrugging without concern. She turned her young womanly wiles in Robert's direction and batted her spiky lashes at him. "I hear they're looking for help at Green Hills, and the trainer's a real dishy guy. Ain't that right, Bobby?"

Braddock wheeled toward his friend with stark panic in his eyes, but Christian took no pity on him. He was too wrapped up in his own worries.

"I'm going to watch the next competition," he mumbled, and wandered off in the direction of the show ring.

It was all that time he'd spent with his family, he thought morosely. They'd rubbed off on him. Three weeks with the Athertons was enough to give anybody a stiff neck. He rubbed the back of his now as he leaned against a light pole and stared, unseeing, at the horse and rider negotiating the jumper course in the arena.

The effect would wear off, he was certain. He would loosen up again. All he needed was a bit of fun with any one of a number of ladies whose names would have rated gold stars in his address book had he been gauche enough to use such a system. He preferred to appreciate every woman for her own unique qualities and leave rating systems to men with no class.

There was Hillary Collins, he reflected. She was always pleasant company. And then there was Regina Worth, who had two *really* outstanding qualities, he thought with a lazy grin. And Louisa Thomas . . .

But each name that came to mind faded quickly away. The truth of the matter was, he didn't feel like seeing any of them. The only woman he was interested in seeing was the one who had turned him down. The one with the flashing amber eyes and sexy, sexy mouth. The one with the mysterious past. The one who had sent him sprawling with the ruthless efficiency of a Ninja warrior. The only woman he was interested in was at that very moment riding into the arena on a horse he wouldn't have wished on his worst enemy.

So maybe it wasn't going to be quite so simple to win this bet, Christian thought as he watched the unflappable Ms. Gianni cast an imperious glance at the course she was about to negotiate, but then he had all the time in the world. It had never taken Christian Atherton a month to get a date with a woman in his life. Alexandra Gianni was not going to be the exception to that rule.

Three

Terminator reared as the arena gate swung closed behind him. Alex calmly forced him forward, driving him with her legs. She had learned very quickly that it did no good to punish him for his bad manners. He tended to take reprimands as a challenge and exacted his revenge with even more outlandish behavior. She had decided the only hope she had for redeeming him was to ignore his little fits and do her best to help him keep his mind on his business.

The horse could jump like a champion. His talent over fences was the only thing that had saved his miserable hide from being made into so many baseballs. If she could get him to concentrate on his job and forget the shenanigans, she might prolong his career and put off his trip to the butcher's for another few years.

With that in mind she urged him into a canter and glanced over the course as she circled him near the gate. Because this was just a schooling show, and most of the horses participating were either young, unseasoned, or simply not good enough to make it on the A circuit, the fences were not terribly high—nothing over four feet. And though the course itself was more complicated than those of the hunter classes that had preceded it, it was still well beneath Terminator's capabilities. He had already been shown at higher levels of competition, but Alex had chosen to restart him and bring him up gradually to the tougher levels as they got to know each other, and as she gained more control over his unbalanced mind.

When she noticed Christian standing outside the ring, his gaze riveted on her, she caught herself straightening in the saddle, bringing her chin up, making half a dozen little adjustments that might impress him. Dammit, she scolded herself as she pointed her horse toward his first fence, there was no room for Christian Atherton in her life, and there was certainly no room for him in her head now. She was going to need every scrap of concentration she possessed to get through this round unscathed.

It took Terminator exactly two fences to decide that the course bored him. He lugged on the bit, doing his best to pull Alex's arms out of their sockets while charging toward each low fence and launching himself flatly over them like a steeplechaser. The battle for control waged throughout their round, and Alex was glad jumpers weren't scored on style and manners, as hunters were. All that mattered was that they get themselves over the fences without knocking anything down, and despite everything, Terminator managed to accomplish his task. They would be coming back for the jump-off and competing this time not only against the other horses that had jumped clean first rounds, but against the clock as well. The horse with the best time and least faults would win.

Christian watched her exit the ring. He was impressed with her riding if not her horse. Beyond being proper in her leg position and seat, she had savvy and style. There was something in that style, in the way she held her head, in the way she brought her horse to the fence and moved him away from it, that prodded at his memory. He wanted to think he'd seen her ride before, and yet he hadn't. Odd. Her name didn't ring a bell, and there had been nothing in their conversation—a conversation held in delightfully close quarters—that had sparked further recognition.

Finally he dismissed the whole idea from his head.

He had never met Alex Gianni. A grin spread slowly across his face. He had never met her before, but he was definitely going to get to know her.

"Looks damn fine on a horse, don't she?"

The graveled voice had much the same effect on Christian as fingernails on a chalkboard. He turned and treated Tully Haskell to the trick he'd learned as a schoolboy at Winchester—looking down his nose at someone who was taller than he.

Haskell was a big man in his forties with an upper body made solid from years of physical work, and a paunch that was the result of a more recent sedentary lifestyle and too much fried food. He had taken up a stance beside Christian, planting himself like an oak tree, and was lighting up a long cigar with a gaudy ruby-studded gold lighter.

Christian eyed the blue ribbon pinned to the pocket of his western-cut shirt with sardonic disdain. "Giving out prizes for obnoxious qualities, are they?" he questioned dryly. "You're destined to be a champion, Tully."

"You're a regular laugh riot, Atherton," Haskell said with a sneer, his fleshy face coloring red from the neck up, as if his shirt collar had suddenly gone too tight on him. He shook his cigar at Christian. "We'll see how hard you laugh when Alex and Terminator start mopping up at the big shows."

"You can't be serious, meaning to send that unhinged animal up against a grand prix course?" Christian shuddered at the thought. The grand prix was the most demanding and most prestigious of all the jumper classes, usually held amidst considerable pomp and pageantry and for big purses. The fences and courses were formidable. It took both a sound mind and a sound body for a horse to take the stress. "What are you trying do, get Alexandra killed?"

"Hardly." A reptilian smile curved Haskell's mouth. "This is just the beginning of a long and mutually advantageous relationship between Alex and me."

Christian gave him a sharp look, his brows drawing together above intense blue eyes.

"Yes, Lordy, she do sit a horse nice," the man drawled, his gaze roaming over Alex as she jogged his horse some distance away. He took a long drag on his cigar and exhaled on a sigh that rang unmistakably in Christian's ears as the first stirrings of desire.

Tully turned back toward him with a maliciously smug gleam in his eyes. "I hear she gave you whatfor in the stable. About time you got put in your place."

"Oh, I know my place, Tully," Christian said coolly. "On top."

He stared at the arena where the grounds crew was raising several fences and taking others down in preparation for the jump-off. "Alexandra and I had a bit of a misunderstanding. Rest assured, we'll work it out."

Haskell turned and jabbed Christian hard on the shoulder with a blunt-tipped forefinger. "You stay the hell away from my trainer, you pompous British prig. She's got better things to do than have you pantin' after her. I know your game, Atherton. Charm them into your bed, and they won't try so hard to beat you in the ring. Well, you can just forget it this time."

Christian coldly eyed the finger pressed to his jacket. Using every bit of his inborn self-control, he reined in his temper, rerouting its energy to the force of his personality so that icy contempt rolled off him in a frigid blast. Haskell, sensing he had crossed a line, took an involuntary step backward, and Christian calmly brushed off the shoulder of his coat.

"Regarding Ms. Gianni," he said formally, his blue eyes blazing as he stared into Tully's florid, fleshy face. "You're not her owner and you're not her father, which, in case you haven't noticed, you are more than old enough to be. You pay her to ride your horses. What she does on her own time is none of your damned business."

Glaring at him, and growing redder by the second, Haskell chewed back a retort. The ring announcer called for the first horse of the jump-off. Tully turned abruptly on his booted heel and stalked off in a cloud of smoke.

"Ill-mannered, ill-bred swine," Christian muttered, scowling after him.

"The horse or the owner?" Robert queried, taking up Haskell's place.

"Both. They deserve each other. Would you believe he actually had the nerve to warn me off?" Christian fumed. "The unmitigated gall!"

Braddock arched a dark brow. "Tully's got his eye on the Italian Iceberg too? Well, I'll be damned. That old tub o' lard!" He laughed in disbelief and tucked his hands into the pockets of the green windbreaker he'd thrown on over his riding coat. Grinning, he nudged his friend with an elbow. "Bet she can't throw *him* over her shoulder."

Christian didn't so much as pretend to smile. "Pray to God for his sake she never has to try."

The words came out in nothing short of a growl, making Braddock's eyebrows climb his forehead again. Christian shuddered and rubbed a hand across his eyes. Maybe he was coming down with something after all: terminal respectability. Defending the honor of young women! Gads.

He cleared his throat and changed the subject. "Hard luck on that vertical, old boy."

"Yeah," Robert said on a sigh of resignation. He stared at the fence in question, a barrier of green-and-white poles placed one above the other to make the jump the highest on the course. His horse had been one of many to bring it down in the first round of the class. Now it had been raised for the jump-off and the approach made more difficult. "I don't think that mare's ready to leave the hunter division," he said reflectively. "The distances throw her. She's always trying to add a stride at the last second."

"She's worried," Christian said with a shrug. "She doesn't trust you because you're letting her try to set herself right, and she's not quite ready to do that. Take her in hand a bit, reassure her."

"You always know how to handle a lady," Braddock drawled, teasing lights sparkling in his dark eyes. "What are you supposed to do when she throws you?"

"Oh, shut up," Christian said with good humor.

They turned their attention back to the ring, where yet another competitor had brought down the green-and-white vertical jump. Christian's gaze slid to the far end of the arena, where Alex was waiting on Terminator.

What did one do after being thrown? One got up and tried again. He had every intention of trying again with Alex, and the sooner the better. There was a wager to be won, a jackass to be shown up, and a lady he wanted to know more about.

Terminator pinned his ears and tried to bite the horse that was leaving the ring. Alex jerked his head aside and scolded him in rapid Italian. The strongly accented words floated to Christian on the gentle spring breeze, and he chuckled. Italian was one of the few useful things he'd learned at Cambridge before being asked to leave after scuttling a professor's punt with the professor still in it.

"What'd she say?" Braddock asked.

"Commenting on the members of his family tree."

"Oh, well, he's obviously Tully's. He bears a striking family resemblance from behind."

They broke into laughter and were immediately caught for posterity on film.

"Carter, what are you doing with that camera?" Robert asked.

Carter Hill glanced up from the array of knobs and switches on his camera and raked back a strand of auburn hair. He was thirty-three, tall and slender, as were all the Hills. He smiled pleasantly, somehow still managing to look like a lawyer even without his pinstripes.

"First show in the new arena and all," he said. "Dad wants plenty of pictures. Too bad we won't get you in the winner's circle this time around, Robert."

Braddock shrugged. "Breaks of the game."

Alex rode into the ring then, and Christian's attention focused on her and on the game men and women had been playing since the days of Adam and Eve. He had a feeling he was going to have to make his own breaks, but as far as he was concerned, both he and Alex would come out winners when all was said and done.

Alex sucked in a deep breath and let it out slowly, nudging her horse into a canter as her body relaxed. She pointed Terminator toward the first fence and cursed herself as a lone thought intruded on her concentration. *This is your chance to show Christian Atherton what you're made of.*

Terminator pricked his ears and launched himself over the fence, realizing belatedly that it was higher than before and required more effort on his part. Alex nearly lost her seat at the unexpectedly high jump he made. By the time they landed, she had her position back and her mind on the matter at hand.

They won it at the green vertical. While the other horses had had trouble managing the sharp turn and sudden acceleration needed to clear it cleanly, diving in on corners and charging fences were Terminator's forte. He left the fence intact and kicked up his heels as he dashed away from it.

Alex laughed and slapped him on the neck. It felt good to win. She'd lost so much in the past couple of years, every small victory was another brick for rebuilding the wall of her self-esteem.

Outside the ring she slid off her horse and handed him to her teenage helpers, the two Heathers—Heather Connelly and Heather Montrose, riding students who were trading work for lessons. She gave the girls instructions for them to cool Terminator down and keep him away from other horses. She wouldn't have charged one girl with the task, but between the two of them they would have no trouble. They threw a bright red woolen cooler over the gelding and led him away.

Congratulations floated to her from passing riders, and Alex smiled her thanks as she pulled her helmet off and shook her hair free.

"What'd I tell you, sweetheart?" Tully Haskell said with a grin. He spread his arms expansively, as if expecting Alex to rush into them.

She couldn't quite keep from frowning at his greeting as heads turned in their direction. "Please call me, Alex, Mr. Haskell," she said quietly, her stomach churning.

He shrugged, smile in place on his mouth but not in his eyes. "Whatever you say, sweet—a—Alex." He jerked a thumb toward the arena. "Let's go get our picture taken."

He offered her his arm, but Alex busied herself with her helmet and crop and walked into the ring beside him, thinking this was really unnecessary. It wasn't as if they'd just won the World Cup. Owners—even overbearing ones like Tully Haskell—didn't get their pictures taken with their riders for winning at schooling shows.

Relax, Alex. Just get it over with, and you can go home to Isabella.

"Where's the trophy?" Carter Hill asked, camera in hand as he looked toward the judge's stand where some sort of commotion was taking place among the half-dozen people gathered there.

Suddenly Christian Atherton emerged from the mob with a triumphant look on his face and a small gold cup in his hands. His steady gaze zoomed in on Alex, magnetism turned up full beam. She froze, mesmerized, amazed. It seemed inconceivable that he could elicit such a response from her with so little effort. That he could excite her, and the excitement made her afraid.

"I've been given the great honor of presenting you with your prize, Ms. Gianni," he said smoothly, wedging himself neatly between her and Haskell. The truth of the matter was he had wrested the trophy away from a nine-year-old girl and then consoled her with a bribe of a dollar. Low but effective.

"That's mine, Atherton," Tully said with all the sulky impudence of a spoiled child. He reached for the cup with greedy hands.

Christian grinned brilliantly as Carter Hill shot a picture. "Then here you are, Mr. Haskell." *And may you choke on it,* he silently added.

He turned his smile back toward Alex. "Congratulations."

"Thank you," she said, quelling the juvenile urge to thumb her nose at him. "I guess Terminator and I get along well enough."

"Yes," Christian said, his own teasing temper responding to the fiery lights in her amber eyes as well as to the challenging tilt of her chin. Gads but she was lovely! That inner flame he had caught glimpses of in the stables burned bright now. She was too caught up in the heady sense of victory to try to suppress it as she had before. He flicked a finger down the short slope of her nose and watched the golden sparks shoot off in her eyes. "Perhaps you can have him ready for the fall steeplechase season."

"Plenty of time for us to win a grand prix or two before then," Alex replied tartly, surprised to realize that she enjoyed sparring with Christian. Her blood was racing in much the same way it did when she was soaring over fences on a fast, powerful horse.

Haskell grunted and hugged his cup to his belly. "See there, hotshot. She'll give you a run for your money."

Christian went on staring down into Alex's amber eyes, reading a rich mix of emotions in their sparkling depths, and he felt his blood heat in answer. His gaze slid to the pouty curve of her lower lip, and a lazy smile curled one corner of his mouth as desire curled low and tight in his groin. "I dare say she will," he murmured silkily.

"Just one more picture, folks?" Carter Hill said, raising his camera.

Tully lifted his trophy and bared his teeth. Alex looked up at Christian, unable to look away. And Christian leaned down and kissed her just as the shutter clicked.

A languid warmth flowed through Alex, swirling first through her head then downward, washing all physical strength with it. It wasn't much of an effort as far as kisses went. It wasn't aggressive or even intimate. It was merely a taste, a brushing of his firm lips over hers. And still it made her weak and dizzy.

Alex told herself it was the shock. She hadn't been kissed in a long time. She hadn't allowed a man near enough to accomplish the task. Christian hadn't asked permission. He'd simply seized the moment and kissed her as if he had every right to.

He didn't have the right. His presumptuousness triggered an old flame of anger, and her own guilt at having enjoyed the kiss for an instant poured gasoline on the fire. She pulled back and slapped him, spewing out a stream of violent blistering Italian while Carter Hill snapped pictures.

Christian laughed, perversely delighted by her temper. She had wanted to melt against him—he was too experienced not to know that. Instead she had given him what he no doubt deserved. His cheek was stinging, but it was nothing compared to the lingering sensation of her lips beneath his. Wonderful. Delicious. Instantly addictive.

"My apologizes, Ms. Gianni," he said smoothly, capturing her wildly gesticulating hands with his. "I'm afraid I lost my head."

Still speaking Italian, Alex muttered that his head wasn't the only thing he should worry about losing if he tried to kiss her again.

"I'll bear that in mind," Christian said, blue eyes dancing. "I'm rather attached to that particular part of my anatomy."

Alex blushed furiously at the sudden realization

that he had understood every word she'd said. Irrational anger burned through her because he hadn't had the grace to tell her he spoke Italian.

"Just don't let it happen again, Mr. Atherton," she said. Tilting her nose up to a haughty angle, she whirled and stormed out of the ring.

"Oh, I can't promise that, Ms. Gianni," Christian murmured, watching her go, admiring the sway of her slim hips. "I can't promise that at all."

Alex stormed around her stall area, flinging things into her gear bag, cursing the day God created man. He should have skipped the first effort, made woman, and called it a day. She was sure everything that was wrong with the world—certainly everything that was wrong with *her* world—could be directly attributed to men. They weren't good for anything except opening jars and reaching things on high shelves . . . and kissing.

She swore long and colorfully as that thought intruded on her tantrum. Her lips were still buzzing from contact with Christian's mouth. She dropped the gloves she was holding and pressed her fingers to her lips, swaying slightly as a strong current of residual desire wafted through her. She could still taste him, warm and fresh and too, too tempting.

The sigh that slid from her lungs was heavy with despair. She couldn't afford to be attracted to Christian Atherton. Nor could she afford to have him make a public spectacle of her, she thought, her anger stirring again, rising to the top of the emotional whirlpool.

Damn him for kissing her that way! Who did he think he was? Royalty?

Actually, he was, if memory served. Alex frowned. There was another reason she couldn't go getting tangled up with him. She would be a fool to think her future might include the wealthy son of an earl, and she was not a fool. She'd stopped being a fool the day Michael DeGrazia had walked out on her.

She had a life to rebuild and a daughter to raise. She seriously doubted Christian Atherton would be interested in any of that. Men of his ilk were concerned with little beyond their own immediate needs and desires. That was just another fact of life she had learned to accept.

Putting the whole subject from her mind, Alex let herself into Terminator's stall to remove his cooler. She double-checked the gelding's cross-ties and left the stall, never turning her back on the horse. He glared at her and tossed his head threateningly.

She didn't like the washy chestnut any better than she liked his owner, but beggars couldn't be choosers. She had come to Virginia with no reputation. She couldn't expect to attract a better class of owners until she had made a name for herself among the affluent hunter-jumper crowd.

That would come with time. She had no doubts about her abilities to compete with the likes of Christian Atherton or Robert Braddock or even the legendary Rodney Jenkins. All she needed was time and a chance to prove herself. That she would have to prove herself on horses like Terminator was not the most pleasant prospect, but that was the way it was.

Latching the bottom door of the box she allowed herself a brief, envious glance at her surroundings. The stables at Green Hills Farm spoke of old money and good taste. The oak stalls were light and roomy. The aisle was wide with a polished cobbled floor. There wasn't a cobweb in sight, and the air smelled of sweet hay and pine shavings and horses that had been groomed to perfection.

The stalls she was renting for the day were in the original barn, but Alex knew the Hills had recently expanded their facilities, building an additional barn with a large indoor arena. After years in the legal profession Hayden Hill had retired and decided to make show horses his full-time hobby. He'd spared no expense, up to and including luring Robert Braddock away from SpruceTree to train for him.

Money. While it may well have been the root of all evil, it was also at the bottom of every successful operation.

Alex had sunk every nickel Michael had given her into setting up her own business on the little farm she'd rented outside of Briarwood. The place was run-down, to put it nicely. None of the buildings had seen a coat of paint in twenty years, and the fences were in a sorry state. Even in its best days it hadn't been able to compete with the likes of Green Hills or Quaid Farm, which was located a hill or two beyond her place.

A shiver of awareness went through her at the thought that Christian Atherton was living just a few fields away from her. A very short distance, but light-years away in terms of status. He would probably turn up his aristocratic nose at the sight of her little ramshackle farm.

"I admit it's not much, but it's a start," she murmured, hugging herself. A fresh start in a place where she had no past. A clean slate.

"We did all right today, didn't we, sweetheart?"

Alex jumped but composed herself so quickly, she was certain Tully hadn't noticed. She tugged at the hem of the baggy black sweatshirt she had put on over her white blouse, trying to push aside the feeling that Haskell's eyes lingered longer than was necessary on the skintight pale gray breeches that encased her thighs.

"Yes, very well, Mr. Haskell," she said, all business. "I was especially pleased with the mare. I have no doubts about her going on to A shows."

"She sure as hell outclassed this bunch, didn't she, sugar?" Haskell patted Alex's shoulder and laughed a laugh that managed to sound more smug than good-natured. Of course, that was Tully Haskell all over. He was a man who had, by hook or by crook, pulled himself up from poverty to prosperity and never failed to remind people of the fact. He seemed to believe it made him superior in some way. Survival-of-the-fittest mentality, Alex supposed.

She shrugged off his touch as casually as she could and watched him lean negligently against the bottom door of the mare's stall. Had he been a horse, Alex would have rejected him as a prospect on the basis of his eyes alone. They were small and cold, hinting at a temperament to match. He wore the blue ribbon his mare had won pinned to his shirt for all the world to see, as if her accomplishments somehow reflected favorably on him.

"Well, this is just a schooling show," Alex reminded him. "Still, I think she'll hold her own in fancier company. She's a very nice mare."

That was an understatement. A Touch of Dutch was world-class. Alex couldn't stop thanking God for sending her this one wonderful horse to work with. If she could have just one like Duchess, she would ride a dozen Terminators and deal with a dozen Tully Haskells and not complain. The sorrel mare was sweet tempered, beautiful, talented, and worth a small fortune. What a man like Tully Haskell was doing with her, Alex couldn't imagine. It was like trying to picture the man with Princess Di on his arm. Completely incongruous.

"Yeah," Tully drawled, extracting a long cigar from the breast pocket of his shirt and rolling it between his fingers in defiance of the many No Smoking signs posted around the barn, "she's a mighty fine mare. And her rider's not too damn shabby, either." Haskell shot her a wink and clamped the cigar between his teeth.

Alex swallowed down the instantaneous rush of revulsion and told herself her employer meant nothing by the remark—he was merely complimenting her on her riding.

The hell he was, she fumed, anger bubbling up inside her. He was flirting with her the way he always flirted with her. She never responded in kind, but that hadn't deterred him yet.

"Thank you, Mr. Haskell," she said coolly, staring down at the toes of her boots. How long was it going to take this cretin to get the message?

"Tully," he scolded in a too-familiar voice. "You just call me Tully, sweetheart, and we'll get on like peas in a pod."

The idea of being a pea in a pod with Tully Haskell was hardly an appealing one. Although he made no move to come closer to her, Alex couldn't quite quell the urge to bolt away from him. Where the hell was Heather—either one of them—she wondered crossly as she unlatched Terminator's door and slipped into the stall, preferring the company of the horse to that of his owner.

Keeping a watchful eye on the chestnut she picked up a brush and applied it briskly to his coat.

"Here's that soda you asked for, Mr. Haskell."

"Thanks, Heather, honey, 'preciate it."

The brush stilled on Terminator's back as Alex looked out of the stall, her straight, dark brows drawing together in suspicion. Haskell accepted the can of soda, looking neither contrite nor annoyed. Heather C. set about her work cleaning tack without giving the man another glance.

You've got to stop being so paranoid, Alex told herself. It was ridiculous to think Haskell had sent the girl on an errand for the sole purpose of getting her alone. Besides, there was virtually no chance of being alone in the barn, what with competitors going in and out continually. She was just wasting energy being nervous, and in view of the amount of work she had to do, energy was the last thing she could afford to waste.

Terminator took advantage of his trainer's lapse in attention, taking a swipe at her arm. Alex jumped out of her trance and scolded herself for being so careless. If the cross ties had been any looser, people could have started calling her Lefty. Where would she and Isabella have been then?

"He's got a lot of fire," Tully observed, perversely pleased by the gelding's nasty attitude.

Alex bit back her opinion as she let herself out of the stall and began packing her equipment in her tack trunk. Terminator would have better served the world as a bag of kibble and a bottle of glue, but owners didn't like to hear that kind of thing from trainers.

"Let me help you with that, honey," Haskell said, reaching for the saddle on the rack at the same time Alex did.

His arms brushed her sides as he reached around her. His paunch bumped against her back. Alex grabbed the saddle and twisted out of his embrace, making sure he got a good poke in the ribs with a stirrup iron as she did so.

"I can get it, Mr. Haskell," she said, struggling to curb her reaction and form a polite smile. "Thank you anyway."

Rubbing his side absently, he gave her a brief scowl, then shrugged as if to say it was her loss. "Well, I've got to be taking off. I'll stop by the farm one day next week."

Choking back the urge to tell him not to bother, Alex managed a nod, then breathed a sigh of relief as Tully swaggered off. She went about her work cursing herself under her breath in Italian all the while and throwing in a couple of colorful words for the odious Mr. Haskell. She had overreacted. She was a ninny. She was a coward. She was a fool.

Tully Haskell was a man. That seemed enough of a curse to heap on his balding head. He didn't mean anything by his flirtation. He was just testing the waters, seeing what kind of reception he would get. Any man would have done the same—curse them all. When the fact finally penetrated his tiny brain that he wasn't going to get any encouragement from her, he would back off.

It was simple, she told herself. She was sending out the right signals. As soon as she had ceased to be a novelty, and as soon as the male population of her professional circle figured out she wasn't interested in fun and games, life would settle down to the kind of quiet routine she wanted for herself and her daughter.

She finished her packing, still muttering to herself in the language she had grown up with. Her grandparents, who had emigrated from Italy to California after the Second World War, had insisted the Gianni offspring speak their native tongue while in their home. Alex still spoke it out of habit around the house and in the stable, much to the delight of her teenage students, who thought it very chic to pick up a word or two themselves.

"I'm finished here, Alex," Heather said, brushing her blond braid back over her shoulder. "Is it okay if I go watch?"

Alex absently waved her away. *"Si, si."*

"Mille grazie!" The girl grinned and bounded for the stable door calling, *"Ciao!"*

Alex smiled and shook her head.

"Bon giorno, Signorina Gianni."

The smooth male voice immediately sent her senses on red alert. Red-hot alert. Responses she'd forgotten she possessed rushed through her—heat and tingling and a strange, giddy pleasure. Alex throttled them guiltily, strangling them into control before she looked up to see Christian standing across the aisle from her, lounging against a stall. He had changed out of his riding clothes to trim, faded jeans, a T-shirt that matched his eyes, and a gold suede jacket that looked butter soft and infinitely touchable.

He looked comfortable and sexy, and that blasted come-hither grin of his invited her to come be comfortable and sexy with him. The worst of it was, a part of her wanted to—badly.

She scolded at him as he sauntered toward her, moving with a lazy, subtle grace that spoke volumes about both his athleticism and his background. His eyes caught hers in their powerful tractor beam, and he let his slow, I-know-how-good-we'd-be-in-bed smile ease across his face.

"Mi fa molto piacere vederLa," he said, his pronunciation smooth and perfectly accented. The words rolled over Alex like the caress of silk.

"Well, I'm not delighted to see you," she replied tartly, stiffening her resolve.

He gave her a sad-hurt look that made her stomach somersault, and lifted his hands in question. *"Perche?"*

"Why? Why!" Alex fumed, taking a step toward him. She lifted an accusatory finger under his nose. "I'll tell you why—" She caught herself just before planting that forefinger on his chest. Control, Alex. Calm, control. No wild emotional outbursts, no show of temper, no show of passion. She pulled her hand back, then flung it downward as she stepped away from him, trying to dodge his magnetic field. "No, no, just go away. *Va al diavolo! Mi lasci in pace, per favore!"*

Christian listened to her order to leave her alone but didn't heed it. He was already far too curious about who this lady was. He wanted to know why she kept yanking back her emotions every time they threatened to melt the ice that surrounded her. He wanted to know why she was so anxious to escape when the spark between them was so obvious and so compelling.

He stepped closer and felt the level of heat between them rise. "Don't be angry with me," he said sincerely, his eyebrows lifting in an endearing look of penitence.

Alex sniffed indignantly, determined not be swayed by his handsome contrition. "I'll be angry if I want. You're not sorry for what you did. You're sorry I slapped you."

"A—well, I expect you're right about that," he admitted with a brilliant grin that invited her to grin back. She didn't. Gads, she was a tough one! That was his best bloody smile! He'd melted more resolves with that grin than he could remember. Sobering, he cleared his throat and apologized in earnest. "Look here, Alex, I'm sorry if I embarrassed you. I didn't mean any harm."

"That doesn't make it all right," Alex muttered, thinking of another wealthy, privileged man who had thought he could get away with anything, too, then make it all better with an apology.

"Then let me make it up to you . . . over dinner? Nick does an excellent *pollo del padrone.*"

"I'll have to try it sometime."

"But not tonight . . ." he said slowly. "And not with me."

"No."

He sighed heavily, as if he were finding this whole thing tiring in the extreme. Fine, thought Alex, let him get bored and lose interest. That was, after all, the plan, she reminded herself while trying to ignore the stirring of disappointment inside her.

"I have to ask myself why," Christian said, his eyes narrowing in speculation as he leaned closer. Alex tried to back away, but once again he had managed to corner her.

"There's the obvious reason," she said, sticking her chin out defiantly. "Maybe I don't like you."

One corner of his mouth hooked upward. "That's not what your kiss told me, darling."

"What did my slap tell you?"

"That you're tempestuous."

"You've got an answer for everything, don't you?"

"No," he murmured. "I haven't a clue about who you really are, Alexandra Gianni. But I mean to find out."

The fear that flashed through her eyes was instantaneous. Alex couldn't stop Christian from seeing it. Damn him! Why couldn't he just accept her rejection and walk away like the half-dozen others who had gone before him?

The predatory gleam in his eyes softened to something warm and curious as he took in the tension in Alex's expression. What a pretty little puzzle she was—fire and ice, arrogance and uncertainty. Without even trying, she was weaving a spell around him, and he had no doubt that she would not have been happy to hear it.

"I'll take a rain check on the dinner," he murmured.

Unable to resist, he bent his head and brushed his lips across hers, again tasting the sweet yearning, the longing to respond, then the abrupt retreat of her emotions. He stepped back quickly and caught the hand she lifted to slap him. Though she resisted, he raised it easily to his lips and kissed her knuckles.

"Until we meet again, darling," he said with a grin, backing gracefully away from her. "*Arrivederci,* Alexandra!"

Four

"Pompous, presumptuous, arrogant . . . *man!*" Alex spat the last word as if it were the vilest of curses.

The rigid tension in her muscles was telegraphed to her horse. Terminator's head came up, and his haunches bunched beneath him as he hopped forward nervously. He snorted and jogged sideways as a rabbit rustled the budding leaves of a low bush along the trail.

Alex spoke to him in a gentle voice, mentally scolding herself for letting her mind wander. When she was on this one's back, there could be no room in her head for thoughts of anything but surviving the excursion. As she had been telling herself for the better part of a day, there should never be any room for thoughts of Christian Atherton, and yet her brain stubbornly persisted in conjuring up his image every five minutes. She chased the apparition away with manufactured anger, wasting another five minutes of time and energy. Damn him anyway.

She wanted only peace, a place to raise her daughter, a chance to establish herself in her profession. It made no sense that men insisted on pursuing her when she made no effort to lead them on. It made no sense that a man like Christian Atherton would look her way twice, let alone steal a kiss from her.

She bit her lip and sighed with no small amount of despair when the tingling sensation of his lips against hers came back to her as real as if it had just happened. She could still taste him, warm and sweet. She could still feel the temptation to lean into him.

Damn him for making her want again! Damn him for awakening needs she would sooner have left behind.

Perhaps the most frustrating thing about this business of attracting men was the fact that she had gone to considerable trouble to make herself *less* noticeable. The waist-long wild mane of black ringlets Michael had delighted in had been shorn off. She no longer wore makeup. The bottles of fragrance she so loved stood unused on her dresser. With the necessary exception of her riding breeches, her clothes were baggy and mannish, enhancing no part of her feminine anatomy. She had made a concerted effort to subdue her naturally outgoing personality, to speak quietly, coolly, evenly, to show little of the hot Italian temper and volatile emotions that ran beneath her surface. She had even shortened her name to its least feminine form.

In short, she was sure she had done nothing to attract or encourage Christian Atherton, and still he had made it clear he intended to pursue her.

Sensing her lack of concentration, Terminator bolted suddenly beneath her. Only lightning reflexes and an excellent sense of balance kept her from being unhorsed. Sawing gently on the reins, Alex rose in the saddle and let the big horse move into a ground-eating canter. She had discovered that Terminator quickly soured on arena work and so had chosen to take him for a gallop in the woods that ran up the hill behind her farmstead. He had earned a day away from fences, and Alex herself had had a longing to escape. That she could never really escape her thoughts or her memories was a reality she didn't care to accept.

With an effort she focused on her horse. He moved with unwavering strength and grace up the old logging trail. The forest they swept through was still half-naked, drab with the dead leaves of last season, but brightening with the new leaves of this one. The air was heavy and sweet with the promise of rain and new growth. Alex breathed deeply of it, letting it fill her lungs and clear her mind . . . and still she thought of Christian Atherton.

Christian eased his horse along the trail. His position was perfect—head up, heels down, back straight—but his mind was elsewhere. On the far side of the hill, to be precise. He didn't have a plan as yet, but he hoped something brilliant would come to him by the time he reached Alex's stable. He had yet to be at a loss for either words or actions around a lovely, intriguing woman.

The taste of her was still lingering on his lips. The memory of that instant when her body had swayed ever so slightly into his was still fresh. So was the memory of her flashing amber eyes, her hot tongue, and the stinging slap she had delivered along with her words. A grin curved his mouth at the thought. The lady had a temper. He suspected the lady had a lot of other equally strong feelings as well, but she seemed determined to keep them on a short rein.

He frowned as he recalled her spontaneous bursts of emotion and the way she had instantly throttled each one. His frown deepened as he thought of the bright smiles that had lit up her face only to be extinguished, doused by the wariness in her eyes.

"Secrets, secrets, Alexandra," he murmured, a strong, undefinable emotion of his own surging through him. "I'm going to learn them all, whether you like it or not."

The two riders broke through the trees at the same time. Christian grinned as he recognized the rider in the scarlet jockey cap and black sweater, then scowled as he recognized the horse. He turned his gray to the right to avoid a collision. Alex and Terminator turned in the same direction, and the pair of them cantered up the slight incline of the high meadow.

The horses drifted toward each other. Terminator

pinned his ears and surged against the bit. Alex hauled back on the reins and cursed under her breath when she got no response for her actions except an increase in speed. Ahead of them lay a mile-long stretch of open field, and Terminator was determined to reach the end of it ahead of the horse running beside him.

"Dammit, Christian, pull up!" Alex shouted. "He thinks it's a race!"

Christian eased the gray back half a length, then a length, but Terminator surged on, faster still, out of control. Rising in his irons, he kicked his gelding ahead, urging him with hands and legs. The gray responded with a burst of speed that brought the two horses even once again.

Alex was leaning back, sawing on the reins with every ounce of strength and determination she had and making no impression on her animal whatsoever. Taking his own reins in his right hand, Christian stretched his left arm out, his fingers grasping for Alex's rein, then curling around it.

"Let him go!" Alex ordered as Christian sat back, his movement pulling the two horses closer together.

Alex frantically tried to pull Terminator the other way, but the chestnut had already changed his course and his mind. He was no longer bent on winning the race but on beating the daylights out of his opponent. Ears flattened, he willingly turned his head in Christian's direction and lunged at the gray.

Christian's startled mount bolted sideways to escape his adversary's teeth, stumbled, and went down, sending Christian sprawling. Alex overbalanced to the right, and Terminator neatly dodged left, ducking out from under her. She hit the ground with a teeth-jarring thud and slowly pushed herself to a sitting position just in time to see Terminator disappearing down the trail for home.

"Damn!" she said, tearing up a clump of grass with her gloved fist and throwing it away.

Christian's mount had righted himself and stood

near the edge of the clearing, alternately grazing and staring at his fallen master with wide eyes. Alex's heart went to her throat as her own gaze fell on Christian. He seemed ominously still.

"Christian?" she called, her voice trembling as she scrambled over to him. She unbuckled the chin strap of her jockey's helmet, which suddenly seemed to be strangling her, and still couldn't get a decent breath.

Christian lay like a mannequin in the grass, unnaturally still. What if he were unconscious? He wasn't wearing a helmet—he might have hit his head or been kicked. What if he were—Alex swallowed hard and refused to finish the thought. On her knees she bent over him looking for blood and bruises. "Christian?"

He opened his eyes and smiled weakly. "I do love how you say my name, darling."

Relief washed through Alex like the waters of a burst dam. And in their aftermath came a tide of anger. She pushed herself to her feet and swore at him in Italian. "You're not hurt at all!"

"Try not to sound so disappointed," he said dryly. He sat up gingerly, mentally assessing the damage. A few aches, no major pains, all extremities attached and working.

"*Madre di Dio!*" Alex flung her hands at him, amber eyes flashing. "I thought you'd been killed!"

"Is that a goal of yours or something?" he questioned suspiciously, rubbing an aching shoulder through his dark leather jacket. "This is the second time I've found myself on the ground because of you. Of course, I wouldn't mind if you were down here with me," he added with a roguish grin.

Alex just growled at him and paced, crossing her arms tightly over her chest.

"I say, you won't be able to talk with your hands tucked up against you."

His teasing earned him a baleful glare. He chuckled. The lady didn't want him to know how badly rattled she'd been at the prospect of his death. It was a start.

"You could thank me for saving your beautiful neck," he suggested, fighting back the grin that threatened when her cat's eyes flashed at him again.

"Saving me? You got me thrown!"

"Yes, well, it appeared that beast of yours was going to run all the way to Maryland. I saved you a long trip home."

"At least I would have had a ride," Alex muttered, staring at the woods and the path that eventually led back to her farm. She had a good mile hike ahead of her.

"You can ride my horse. I'll walk. We'll go to your place, since it's nearer," Christian said as he started to get up. Planting his right foot, he winced, sucked in a breath through his teeth, and sank back down to the ground. There was a definite strain in his voice when he said, "Check that. I'm afraid I won't be able to play the gallant after all."

Alex's heart leapt into her throat again as she hurried over to him, forgetting all about cool restraint and suppressing her emotions. "What is it? Is something broken?"

"Ankle," he barked between held breaths. Gradually the pain subsided to a vicious throb, and the rest of his body relaxed. "I must have twisted it in the fall."

Guilt and anger warred inside Alex. He had been trying to save her from a possible disaster, but he wouldn't have gotten hurt if he had stayed out of her life altogether. Blast it, she hadn't asked for him to take an interest in her. Nor had she asked for the tender feelings and the longing to comfort that blossomed within her now.

"Be a love and help me get the boot off before the swelling makes it impossible," he said.

"Are you sure?" she asked, hesitantly taking his foot in her hands. "It'll hurt."

"Not as bad as having to cut it off. These are my favorite boots."

Not to mention expensive, Alex thought, eyeing the softly polished black leather. She could have paid a month's feed bill with what these boots cost, and they were just his everyday pair.

"Hang on," she said, biting her lip for his pain as she tried to pull the boot off. He paled visibly as he strained backward. Sweat filmed his forehead. The knee-high boot didn't budge.

"Hold it. Hold it," he said, gasping. "I need to brace against something. Turn around."

Alex gave him a skeptical look, but turned her back to him, leaned over, and took hold of his foot again, holding it between her slightly spread legs.

"That's it," Christian said. "If nothing else, the view is exceedingly fine."

"On three," Alex muttered, not liking the leap in her pulse at his comment about her derriere. "One . . . two . . ."

He planted his other foot on the seat of her breeches, sucked in a deep breath, and pushed hard as she called three and pulled at the reluctant boot. Pain exploded in his ankle and shot up his leg like an electric current, but the boot came free. The easing of the pressure and the cool spring air immediately soothed the injury.

Christian leaned back on his elbows, panting, his hair falling rakishly across his forehead. Relief allowed him to smile up at Alex.

"Was it as good for you?" he asked breathlessly.

Alex scowled at the sexy, tempting picture he presented, tossed his boot at him, and knelt down. She peeled his sock off and gingerly examined the ankle that had already begun to puff up. With gentle hands she felt for any sign of a broken bone and found none.

"Please feel free to do that to any other part of me," Christian said, his voice a low sensual purr. Pain or no, he was enjoying the feel of her small capable hands on his flesh. He groaned a little under his breath as her ministrations called to mind the particularly erotic dream he'd had about her the night before.

"I ought to leave you for dead," Alex grumbled, trying to ignore the heat in her cheeks and the sudden sensitivity in her nipples.

"If you do that, then you won't be able to go to dinner with me this evening."

"I'm not going to dinner with you regardless," she said firmly, looking him straight in the eye. "I'm not getting involved with you."

Christian looked hurt. "How can you say that after you've fondled my foot? What kind of fellow do you take me for?"

"You don't want to know."

"Sure I do." Leaning forward he caught her wrist as she tried to move away. She stiffened immediately, her dark eyes going wide with an instinctive fear reaction she couldn't mask. Her involuntary response tugged at his curiosity and his heart. "I want to know all about you, Alex," he said gently, his fingers rubbing soothingly against the fragile skin of her wrist, feeling the pulse that raced there.

Alex stared at him, her heart pounding. She felt like a rabbit caught in a snare. Christian was watching her with his steady blue gaze. He was far too close. She could feel the magnetic power of him, luring her, tempting her to close the distance between them. Her mouth tingled at the memory of his kiss. Unconsciously she ran her tongue across her full lower lip. Finally his words penetrated. *I want to know all about you.*

"No," she whispered, pulling away from him. "No, you don't."

Confused and upset, she rose unsteadily to her feet and went to catch the gray gelding. The horse came to her willingly, trustingly, obediently, and she spared a singularly nasty thought for the bag of dog chow that had left her stranded. Faithlessness was just another of Terminator's long list of unattractive traits.

Christian managed to mount with some difficulty.

After he'd settled himself in the saddle, he sat for a long minute with his eyes squeezed shut, fighting off the screaming pain in his ankle. When it subsided, he managed a tepid version of his rogue's smile for Alex and patted the limited space in front of him on the jumping saddle.

"You can ride with me," he invited, knowing she would refuse him.

Just the idea of being that close to him gave Alex a hot flash. She could too vividly imagine the feel of his strong arms around her, of her breast flattening against the solid wall of his chest, and her hip pressing intimately against his groin as she sat sideways in front of him. Angry with herself and her traitorous hormones, she merely shot him a scowl and set off on foot down the path toward her farm.

Christian watched her stride off with his boot in her arms, and he couldn't help but think she was running away. But from what? He meant to find out. Sooner or later, one way or another, he would find out.

"Lord, Alex, you had me scared out of my wits!" Pearl Washington exclaimed as Alex trudged into the yard.

Pearl's dark round face was lined with worry over the natural creases of sixty-eight years of living. Balancing Isabella on one plump hip, she pressed her free hand to her ample bosom and heaved a sigh of relief. "That devil came galloping back here all by himself. I could only think the worst. This poor child left motherless. Lord have mercy." She shook her head for emphasis.

"You've got cause to worry when she goes out on that one, Pearl," Christian said, sliding carefully off his horse. Alex scowled at him and hit him in the stomach with his boot as she handed it to him. His breath left him with an "oof."

"It was just a minor crash. Christian twisted his ankle, but I'm fine," Alex said. Terminator stood some distance away, near the barn. She glared at him, then turned with a smile to take her daughter.

"Mama," Isabella said, grinning, attaching herself to her mother's side like a limpet. Her attention was immediately snared by the swinging strap of Alex's helmet. She wrapped a chubby hand around it and stuck the end in her mouth. Alex fondly tousled her daughter's black curls and kissed her cheek.

When she had moved to Virginia, she had feared she would have to put Isabella in day care. Both the idea of the cost and the thought of separation had upset her. But it seemed fate had been smiling down on her for a change. She had found Pearl Washington. Or more accurately, they had found each other.

Pearl, a recent widow, had been looking for a renter and some new meaning in her life. She had retired from her job as an elementary-school secretary, planning to spend her time with her husband. Then Rube had died suddenly, leaving her bereft. Alex had needed a stable and care for her ten-month-old daughter. Pearl had gladly rented her the place and had simply stayed on in the house, filling her days with caring for Isabella. It was the ideal arrangement for both of them.

"Do I get an introduction to this charming young lady?" Christian asked, leaning close so the baby could get a good look at his face.

"This is my daughter, Isabella."

"What a lovely name. Isabella." The baby dropped the chin strap and stared at him. He smiled beguilingly, figuring a female was a female. "Hello, Isabella," he murmured. "What a pretty little girl you are."

"Don't feel bad if she starts to cry," Alex said. "She doesn't like—"

Her daughter didn't give her a chance to finish the sentence. With a little squeal she let go of her mother and launched herself at Christian, who caught her up against his chest.

"—men," Alex said lamely, her dark brows drawing together in confusion.

Isabella seldom went to strangers and *never* to a strange man, perhaps picking up on her mother's sense of caution. But she certainly looked happy in Christian's arms, smiling her cherubic little smile as he whispered in her ear, amusing herself with the zipper of his leather jacket. Alex could only stare in stunned disbelief, as baffled by Christian's ease as she was with her daughter's. He didn't strike her as the daddy type at all. He didn't even strike her as the marrying type. She would have bet the only thing he knew about babies was how to make them.

"Don't look so surprised, darling," Christian said, looking at her from under his lashes. "Women, with the notable exception of yourself, always like me."

Alex pressed her lips into a thin line and reached for the gray's reins. "I'll see to the horses."

Christian watched her walk away, chuckling a little under his breath.

Pearl snorted. "Laugh now, Mr. Atherton. You've got your work cut out with that one. She's not one of your flighty little fillies for chasing around with."

"Yes, ma'am," he said, giving the older lady his best contrite-little-boy look. He watched her stern glower melt into a laugh that lit up her round face.

"And she's got her work cut out for her, I can see that! Lordy!" She reached for the baby. "Get yourself inside the house, boy. I'll see to that ankle and give you a piece of cherry pie if you're good."

"I'm *always* good," Christian said with just enough suggestiveness to make the woman cluck at him and shake her head with reproach that didn't reach her twinkling eyes.

"Poor Miss Alex," she muttered, heading up the cracked walk to the simple old farmhouse.

Christian glanced around the yard as he hobbled toward the house, taking in the general state of the place. The house itself didn't look too decrepit. Daffodils and tulips were pushing themselves up through the ground along the front porch, lending cheer. The rest of the buildings had not fared as well over time. The stable leaned decidedly to one side. What little paint was left on it had long ago turned from white to dingy gray. The board fences around the small paddocks looked no better. More than one board was held to its post by baling twine. Many of the posts tilted drunkenly.

The place was quiet. Nothing marred the stillness but the occasional bang or nicker coming from the stable and the paddocks adjacent to it. Judging by the size of the barn and the number of animals in the pens, he would have guessed Alex was caring for fifteen to twenty horses. By herself. There was no sign of hired help around.

There were no signs of prosperity either. The dull yellow horse van parked near the barn had to be nearly twenty years old. It looked as though someone had taken a chain to it. Even at that, it appeared to be more roadworthy than the blue '77 Impala that was parked nearer the house, next to Pearl's little red Escort. The tires were almost bald. One back window was missing, the opening covered over with clear plastic and duct tape. All in all, it looked as unsafe as Terminator. He shuddered at the thought of Alex driving it on the area's winding roads.

It was clear to him she needed money. She claimed money was the reason she had taken on Tully Haskell and Terminator. But there were simpler, safer answers to her dilemma. She was a top-notch rider. She would have had no trouble getting hired on at any good stable, including Quaid Farm. She had chosen instead to start her own place and run it on the proverbial shoestring. And a worn, frayed shoestring it was. He couldn't help but wonder why.

"Get along in here now," Pearl scolded from the porch. "I can't be keeping this baby out in the breeze. She'll be up all night with an earache, and where will you be? Long gone, that's where."

He watched the woman disappear into the house, and he hobbled after her, thinking that if anyone around Briarwood knew about Alexandra Gianni and her mysterious past, it would have to be Pearl.

*　　*　　*

An hour later Christian was sitting in the cab of the horse van with a numbing bag of ice on his ankle, heading up the winding road toward Quaid Farm, none the wiser about the petite woman wrestling with the oversize steering wheel of the truck. Pearl had proved to be as reticent as a clam when it came to doling out information about the young woman with whom she was sharing her home. If she knew any of Alex's secrets, she hadn't been willing to pass them along to him. It seemed he was going to have to go to the source.

"Where did you say you came from?" he asked conversationally. "I can't seem to place you by your accent."

"I haven't got an accent," Alex said evasively. "You have an accent."

"Not according to anyone in Wessex."

Ball to Gianni's court. Alex would have shot him a look if she hadn't needed all her concentration on the twisting road that was growing slick with mist.

"What brought you to the States?" she asked, turning the tables on him. "Show jumping is so big in Britain. I'm sure you could have done well there with your own stable."

"Hmmm," Christian said noncommittally. He could have done well, but he had been interested by neither the responsibility nor the idea of working under the jaundiced eye of those in his family who thought riding was a proper hobby for a gentleman but not at all suitable as a profession.

"It's a long story," he said at length, surprised at the thought that he might just like to share that story with Alex. He ordinarily had no desire to discuss such complex emotions with a woman, preferring to keep things light and fun. But he had a feeling Alex would be sympathetic. He gave her a beguiling, crooked smile. "I might be persuaded to tell it over a nice plate of scampi with red sauce."

Alex couldn't help but laugh. He was charmingly

persistent. She actually felt tempted for the first time in a long time. Hunger stirred inside her at the thought of a cozy restaurant, an excellent meal . . . and Christian sitting across the table from her. Warm, sweet yearnings fluttered through her like ribbons in a slow breeze, stirring, tempting . . . dangerous to her. Her hands tightened on the steering wheel as common sense reminded her of her need for caution, her need for independence.

"I don't think I like the way your chin is lifting up," Christian said wryly, tilting his head back against the cracked vinyl seat of the van. "Bodes ill for my dinner plans, I'd say."

Glancing across at him Alex smiled at the comical expression of disappointment he wore. She doubted he lacked for dinner companions or companions of any sort. She was just a challenge to him. "I'm not going to go out with you, Christian."

"I'm not going to stop asking," he said pleasantly, but his sophistication suddenly seemed like a highly polished veneer over a core of raw masculine determination. "Never surrender and all that," he added lightly.

Alex clucked her tongue and shook her head as she turned her attention back to the road. "Just think of all the lovely ladies you could be going out with while you waste your time on me."

"You're the only lady I'm interested in, Alex," he murmured, suddenly serious.

The cab of the horse van seemed to shrink. Alex was acutely aware of the man sitting beside her, of his compelling personality, of the scent of his leather jacket, and the feel of his steady gaze.

"I mean to woo you, Alexandra," he said, managing to call back some of his usual lightheartedness. He crossed his arms over his chest casually and flashed her a roguish grin. "And if I do say so myself, I'm damned good at it."

"I don't doubt that you're the world champion," Alex said sardonically. "But you're going to knock yourself out this time."

"We'll see."

Mercifully the road changed the topic for her. "Is this the turn?"

"Yes."

Alex hit the blinker, slowed the van, and shifted down, grinding the gears horribly as they turned and started up the gravel drive. They drove up and around a thickly wooded hill, finally emerging at the top where pastures rolled before them like an emerald quilt, each square delineated by dark, four-plank oak fencing. The large white sign at the end of the first field read Quaid Farm in simple, elegant royal blue letters.

The pang of envy was automatic. This was what she had always dreamed of—the long, tree-lined drive, the pastures dotted with top-quality stock, the immaculate white buildings. It was what she had left behind. Now it would be a long time before she would be able to drive up a lane like this one and feel as if she were something other than a delivery person.

"Pull up at the first barn," Christian said.

Alex did as instructed, taking in as much of the place as she could while she parked and shut down the van, ignoring the way the engine ran on, knocking and clanking. There were two long stables with the big end doors rolled back, revealing rows of brightly lit box stalls. The first barn was attached to a large indoor arena. Farther away stood a smaller barn with brood mares waiting patiently in the paddocks, and another low white building that was probably the breeding shed. Off to the right, beyond a small yard strewn with toddler's toys, stood the house, a larger, better-maintained version of the one she was renting. It was a typical old-fashioned Virginia farmhouse with a welcoming porch and a shiny tin roof, and windows full of warm light and lace curtains.

The stable yard was bustling with activity as afternoon chores began. Stable hands moved energetically from one building to the next, each of them followed by at least one dog. The dogs were of all sizes and breeds, and they trotted purposefully along, as if they felt their presence was necessary for the men to do a proper job.

Rylan Quaid sauntered to the doorway of the first barn as Alex climbed down out of the cab of her truck. She recognized him from photographs in the horse magazines. His was one of the most ambitious breeding programs in the country as far as jumping horses went. His younger sister Katie had once been one of the top young riders on the circuit, destined for a spot on the Olympic team, when a fall ended her career and nearly ended her life.

Alex looked up at the owner of Quaid Farm and swallowed hard. If he had looked unapproachable in his photographs, he looked downright intimidating in the flesh. He was a huge man, six feet four and built like a bull. His face looked to be carved of granite, an appropriate pinnacle for a mountain of masculinity. His features were rough-hewn and angular. He seemed physically incapable of smiling. Narrow, stormy eyes stared at her from beneath heavy dark brows.

"Alex, this cantankerous looking person is Rylan Quaid."

Alex jumped at the sound of Christian's voice so near her ear. He had slid across the seat of the van and eased himself to the ground beside her.

"Ry, this is Alexandra Gianni, the trainer I was telling you about."

"It's a pleasure, miss," Ry said, politely touching the bill of his battered blue baseball cap. He swung immediately in Christian's direction, piercing his friend and trainer with a fierce look of annoyance. "Jeepers cripes, Atherton, where the hell have you been? I've got Bobby and Marlin up in the woods looking for your body."

"Metallica and I took a bit of a tumble, I'm afraid," he explained as Alex went around to the back of the van. "Alex rescued me."

Alex led the gray gelding down the ramp of the

van and into the aisle of the barn. Scowling, Ry immediately bent to inspect the animal's legs for damage.

"He's fine," Christian said, hobbling into the barn with his boot in one hand and his ice bag in the other. "I didn't fare as well. Thanks for asking."

Ry turned his scowl at him, rising up to his full height and planting his hands at the waistband of his faded jeans. "You're hurt? How the hell can you be hurt? You're like a damn cat—always land on your feet."

Christian lifted his stockinged foot. "Well, I won't be landing on this foot for a while. I've twisted my ankle."

"I think we ought to shoot him, don't you, gov'nor?" Charlie asked, coming to take the horse. "Put him out of his mis'ry like. Right?"

Christian frowned at the girl as he felt his blood pressure shoot up. "You are perpetually insubordinate," he said through his teeth.

Charlie squinted and laughed her carefree laugh, shaking a finger at him. "My, aren't we stuffy today? Stuffy, stuffy."

"I'll give you stuffy," Christian growled, leaning over her aggressively. "Take that horse and groom him till he shines like sterling, or you'll have the devil to pay."

"Go on. Go on. Cuff me one," Charlie challenged teasingly, turning her round, rouged cheek to him for a target. "Box me a good one right here in front of all these nice witnesses. I'll sue your bloody bum off. That nice Mr. Hill is a solicitor, you know. I'll go straight to him."

Ry's face cracked into a smile at the shade of red Christian was flushing. "Go on along now, girl," he said to Charlie. "Get to work before he takes you up on it."

Alex watched the scene through cautious eyes, wondering if Christian was capable of that kind of violence.

"So, hotshot," Ry said. "You need a lift to the hospital?"

"I don't need a doctor," Christian said, watching Alex edge back toward the door of her truck. She was ready to make her getaway, but he wasn't anywhere near ready to see the last of her. "It's just a sprain. I'll be all right to ride"—he broke off and just managed to suppress a grin at his own genius—"in a week or two."

Rylan heaved a strained sigh and rubbed a big hand across the back of his thick neck. "Jeepers cripes. We can't afford to lay off. Diamond Life is just coming into form. Legendary is finally getting it all together. Bobby can school the young horses, but with Greg gone to Germany . . . well, hell."

"I was thinking perhaps we could get Alex to ride for us until I'm fit." Christian turned to her with one of his dazzling smiles. She was looking at him as if he had just pulled the dirtiest of tricks. "She's excellent. I wouldn't have any qualms about having her."

Alex blushed furiously at the double meaning that was obvious in his mischievous gaze as he grinned down at her.

"What do you say, Ms. Gianni?" Ry asked, oblivious to the undercurrents surging between the two trainers. "Chris tells me you're top-notch. We've got a show string needs riding every day if we're gonna have them ready for Devon."

The Quaid Farm show string. A sharp pang of longing went through Alex's chest. He was talking about horses that made most of hers look like an inferior species. But she didn't want to work for someone else, she reminded herself. The last thing she wanted was to have to answer to Christian, who had set his sights on her like a hawk swooping down on a field mouse. Besides, she had horses of her own to ride. She was working twelve-hour days that left her little energy for anything extra.

"I'm afraid I already have a full schedule, Mr. Quaid," she said with a mix of relief and regret.

"If you had a good groom working for you, you'd have sufficient time to ride at least my grand prix horses as well as your own," Christian said.

Alex stuck her chin out and gave him a steady stare. "But I don't have a groom."

"You ought to have," he insisted, that unfamiliar feeling of responsibility rearing its ugly head again. He didn't want Alex working like a dog. She was too small and fragile. "You will have if I loan you Charlie," he said, smiling as he thought of killing two birds with one stroke of genius.

"I couldn't let you do that."

"It's not as big a favor as you think," he said dryly. "She's going to drive me mad. I'd be more than happy to send her to you and pay her room and board as well as her salary."

"I don't need your charity," Alex said stiffly, her obsessive sense of self-reliance asserting itself. She depended on no one. She had leaned on others for support before, and they had stepped away when she'd needed them most, letting her fall on her face. She had been forced to learn to stand on her own two feet. If she let Christian have his way, she doubted she'd be left standing at all.

Ry snorted. "Hell, girl, that ain't charity, it's business. We need a rider. If we have to trade you a groom on the deal, so be it—as long as Charlie agrees."

"But—"

Cutting to what he felt was the heart of the matter, Ry named a figure for a week's work that made Alex's head swim. She'd forgotten what a good stable could afford to pay. Temptation battered her resistance. The chance to ride world-class horses and get paid handsomely for it. Could she really afford to turn the offer down? Did she really want to?

"Well, that's settled then," Christian said cheerfully, his smile brilliant enough to light the darkening day. He wrapped an arm companionably around Alex's slim shoulders, not missing the way she stiffened at his touch. She shot him a warning glance but didn't try to pull away. His voice dropped automatically to a seductive purr. "Alex, let's you and I go discuss the particulars—say, over a nice glass of wine?"

Ry rolled his eyes and muttered, "I should have guessed." Clearing his throat he offered a big callused hand to Alex and said, "Thanks for helping us out, Ms. Gianni. I appreciate it."

"You're welcome," Alex said, surprised at how gentle his grasp was when he was certainly capable of cracking coconuts with it. She noticed then that his hard looking gray green eyes had softened subtly and his smile was warm. There was no doubt a very nice man under the gruff exterior, she realized.

A skinny tow-headed groom interrupted them, clearing his throat nervously as he came out of the office. "Mr. Quaid, sir? Mrs. Quaid just called and says you're needed up at the house."

Ry instantly turned gray. He bolted out of the barn and across the yard through the thickening mist.

Alex lifted a questioning brow as Christian chuckled.

"His wife is expecting their second child," he explained. "He worries about her incessantly, even though it isn't necessary. Maggie is as healthy as a horse."

"How sweet," Alex murmured. A sense of loss assailed her as she watched Ry bound up the steps of his porch and charge into the house. Michael had never worried about her or fussed over her during her pregnancy. He had avoided her, watching her from a distance with hurt and guilt and accusation in his dark eyes. And finally he had divorced her, not able to wait it out, giving in to the pressure before he'd even had the chance to see or hold the daughter who ironically looked just like him.

Christian studied her expression, the need to hold and console her stealing upon him again. He didn't curse it quite as strongly as he might have. It seemed only civilized to feel protective toward a woman with such a terrible, haunted look in her eyes. He couldn't begin to imagine what could have happened to put such a look there. All he could think of was doing his best to erase it.

"Let's go have that drink," he said softly.

Why she went with him, Alex couldn't have said. The idea of going into the lion's den to share his hospitality ordinarily would have set off a cacophony of warning bells. Not this time. She told herself it was because Christian was injured. She could out-run him if necessary. Deeper down she suspected it had something to do with the quiet comfort he'd offered in his cultured British voice and warm blue eyes.

Curiosity played a part as well. What rider wouldn't have wanted to see how Christian Atherton lived?

His cottage sat on a well-tended lawn away from the main house and on the opposite side of the drive, a short walk from the stables, though they took Alex's van because of Christian's lack of mobility. As soon as they were in the front door he dropped onto a deep green overstuffed sofa and eased his aching leg up on the matching footstool.

The room was impeccably decorated in a masculine English country style with shades of dark red, beige, and hunter green throughout. The floor was old polished pine with a thick beige area rug covering most of the space. Fox-hunting scenes decorated the walls. The furniture looked antique. The overall effect was of expensive tastes and a comfortable lifestyle.

"I'm afraid I'm not going to be much of a host," Christian admitted ruefully.

His ankle was throbbing something fierce, hurting worse than he had thought it would. Damn, he thought darkly, he had Alex in his lair but no strength to take advantage of the situation. Bloody rotten luck. Of course, the silver lining was the thought of having her at the farm every day for a week. He brightened at the prospect.

"There's a bottle of white zinfandel in the fridge, if you don't mind playing hostess."

"I shouldn't have any. I have to drive home. With these roads and the rain . . ."

"And that truck," Christian muttered under his breath. Fighting off the respectable urge to lecture her on safety, he cleared his throat and nodded. "Quite right. Be a love, though, and bring me a glass, would you? It tastes a far sight better than aspirin."

"Sure."

The way to the kitchen was obvious. Alex went through the archway between the living room and dining room, passed an elegant mahogany dining set that looked older than the United States, and went into the kitchen beyond. The wine in the refrigerator was expensive, the glasses in the cherry-wood cupboard crystal.

She treated herself to a sip of the blush-colored wine, moaning in appreciation at the crisp, fresh taste. Good wine was something she couldn't afford to indulge in these days.

As she returned to the living room she glanced down a hall that led presumably to the bedroom. Something basically feminine in her fluttered with curiosity about what she might find in there. Scolding herself for caring, she hurried on.

"Is there anything else I can get you?" she asked, handing him his drink. "I really should be going. I have chores to do yet tonight."

"Sit for a minute," he said, nodding to the empty end of the couch, amazed when she obeyed. He took a drink, closed his eyes, and sighed reverently, then set the glass aside on an antique pine end table. "I haven't thanked you for offering to help."

"I didn't offer," Alex said sardonically. "You rail-roaded me."

Christian gave an imperious shrug. "A minor detail. I really do appreciate it, Alex. Besides, it seemed only sporting since you're the one who got me thrown in the first place."

He chuckled as her eyes flashed, and she sucked in a breath in prelude to what was undoubtedly a scathing opinion of his version of the accident. She didn't let the words out, though her face went red with the effort to hold them back.

He was fast discovering all the right buttons to push, Christian thought, feeling a bit smug. Very soon Alex was going to have to give up all pretense of hiding her emotions from him. He liked that idea very much.

"I'd better go," she said stiffly.

Trying to ignore the pain in his ankle, he rose and escorted her to the door, hobbling and wincing all the way.

Alex pulled the door open and groaned aloud at the sight of the strong, steady rain that had begun to fall and the expanse of yard she had to run across to get to her truck.

"Don't suppose you'd rather stay till it lets up?" he said dryly. "I can think of any number of ways for us to pass the time."

Alex gave him a look. "I'll bet."

She was amazed that she didn't feel an urgent need to escape him. The need to escape her own awakening desires was another matter altogether, but Christian . . . He was smiling at her—one of his lopsided, I'm-your-best-friend smiles—his fathomless blue eyes twinkling with good humor. How many other men would have been petulant over her constant rebuffs? She could name one in particular, one other wealthy, handsome, privileged son. . . .

The thought drifted away as Christian leaned forward and kissed her. He didn't try to hold her. He hung on to the open door with one hand and braced the other against the jamb. He touched her only with his mouth, and she responded without thought, tilting her head back. He tasted warm and as intoxicating as the wine that lingered on his lips.

Lifting his head, he murmured, "Drive carefully, darling. I'll see you in the morning."

Stunned by her own reaction, Alex said nothing. She just turned and ran from the house to the sanctuary of her decrepit yellow truck. Once inside the cab she sat clutching the steering wheel with white-knuckled hands, listening to the rain pound down on the roof. And she wondered what the hell she'd just gotten herself into.

Five

This had to be what it was like to ride Pegasus, Alex thought dreamily as she and Diamond Life soared over an array of red-and-white bars. The young Hanoverian stallion launched himself effortlessly over the fence and practically floated back to earth. Alex's spirit stayed somewhere in the stratosphere. This was what riding jumpers was all about. To glide and sail on the back of a powerful, willing animal.

It was only her first ride on the blood bay that was Quaid Farm's heir to the throne of their great jumper Rough Cut, the horse that had set a bookful of records and then been retired to stand at stud, and already she was thoroughly in love with him. He was talented, obedient, enthusiastic—in short, Diamond Life was everything most of her mounts were not. He shared a sire with Rough Cut and showed every intention of taking his sibling's place in the arena.

Sadly, Rough Cut would never be in a position to challenge the young bay. Upon his retirement he had been stricken with a devastating illness that had left him chronically lame and sterile. Time and extensive, often experimental, treatment had solved the second problem. He seemed perfectly happy in his role as daddy, seemingly not missing the exquisite grace and speed that had won him fame the world over. He was kept comfortable with painkillers and spent his time out of the breeding shed dozing contentedly in a large paddock that faced the Blue Ridge mountains.

Diamond Life was the up-and-coming star of Quaid Farm and the grand prix circuit, and Alex was more than enjoying the experience of schooling him. She took him around the spacious indoor arena, over a series of jumps known as a gymnastic, designed to improve a horse's rhythm and form, then cantered him diagonally across the ring, popping him over a small vertical and then a spread fence. Each one was perfection and joy.

Christian watched from the gate that led into the barn, his admiration plain on his face. He may have been a flatterer by nature, but he never gave false praise to a rider. Flirting was one thing, riding was serious business. One had to earn respect in the show ring, and Alex had his. It was ridiculous how proud that made him feel. Shaking his head a little, he decided he was behaving like an infatuated schoolboy.

"She's good, isn't she?" Maggie Quaid asked.

Christian glanced down at her and smiled warmly. Maggie had stolen his heart four years ago when she'd asked him to help her overcome her fear of horses so she could spend more time with Ry. Sassy and flirtatious, Maggie had a heart of pure gold. She doted on her friends and adored her irascible husband. Rylan worshiped the ground she walked on.

"How are you feeling today, Maggie?"

She patted her well-rounded belly and made a face. "Like a minivan."

"Oh, you're beautiful and glowing, and well you know it."

She tilted her head so her red bob fell at a flattering angle along her jawline and batted her lashes at him. "Why, Mr. Atherton," she said, her voice pure magnolias and honey, "how you do go on."

Christian chuckled and turned back toward the arena. "To answer your question: Yes, she's very good."

"She must be something special to keep your feet on the ground."

"In case you hadn't noticed," he said dryly, leaning back to display his crutches, "I *am* injured."

"Mmm-hmmm," Maggie murmured, unimpressed by his props. "Like you were injured that time a whole herd of yearlings trampled you and you won the Cavalier Classic the next day?"

He scowled at her sweet, brown-eyed smile. "That was entirely different."

"Oh, you're quite right. That time you had three cracked ribs, bruised kidneys, and a mild concussion."

His scowl darkened, the aristocratic lines of his face sharpening.

"And you didn't have a pretty, black-haired little gal to take your place so you could spend time trying to charm her." Maggie put an arm around his lean waist and gave him an affectionate hug. "Don't try to outfox me, sugar. I know every trick in the book."

He considered asking her to share a few with him, but the day hadn't come when Christian Atherton needed to ask advice about wooing a lady. He shored up his pride and held his tongue.

They watched Alex for another moment, chatting companionably as she and Diamond Life worked in the empty end of the ring, moving laterally, cantering in concentric circles that grew smaller and slower, then larger and faster. Finally she slowed the horse to a walk and pulled off her helmet, shaking her hair free in the gesture that seemed hauntingly familiar to Christian.

"Look at all that hair," Maggie murmured. "Think if it were long, how wild it would be."

Christian grew still as he tried to capture the ghost of a memory floating through his mind. A petite young woman with a long mane of untamed black ringlets and a bright red blouse that stood out like fire against her olive complexion. He could just see her tossing her head back in that certain way.

But he couldn't quite place the memory, and he couldn't place Alex.

"How was that?" Alex asked as Diamond Life sauntered lazily toward the gate.

"Smashing." Christian grinned. "How do you like him?"

Alex rolled her eyes and offered her highest praise in heartfelt Italian. As a groom came into the ring and took the horse by the bridle, she hopped to the ground and began unfastening the girth.

"I'll see to that, Ms. Gianni."

"Right." Alex nodded sheepishly. The days of riding and walking away, leaving the dirty work to someone else, had all but faded from her memory. It was a nice treat. But she couldn't get used to it, she reminded herself sternly.

"You look wonderful on him," Maggie said as Alex let herself out the gate. "I'm Maggie Quaid."

"I'm pleased to meet you, Maggie, and thanks. But I think Diamond Life could make anybody look good. He's a fabulous animal."

"You've obviously never seen me ride," Maggie said dryly.

There was a sudden commotion in the alleyway, and from around the corner of a stall appeared a sturdy dark-haired little boy of about three leading a big white goat with a length of twine. The goat was protesting loudly. The boy leaned ahead and trudged along as if he were towing a barge, the determined look on his face a miniature version of his father's scowl.

Alex covered her laughter with her hand. Christian tightened his lips against his.

Maggie rolled her eyes. "Buddy, let that goat be. Buddy . . ."

The toddler and the goat faced-off in a tug of war.

"Thomas Randall Quaid," Maggie snapped. "Leave that animal alone."

Buddy Quaid didn't have a chance to disobey his mother's dictate. The goat lunged forward suddenly, knocked him on the seat of his miniature blue jeans, and scampered out into the arena, its tether floating behind it like a ribbon.

"See what happens when you don't listen to your mama?" Maggie said gently, leaning down to help her son up and dust off his britches.

Buddy's face was a study in disappointment. His lower lip jutted forward threateningly. "Darn goat."

"Don't you worry about the goat, young man. You worry about what your daddy's going to say if he catches you trying to ride that creature again. He's told you a hundred times you can't ride goats."

Buddy scuffed the toe of his little cowboy boot against the concrete and looked dejected. Maggie's stern expression melted, and she pressed a kiss to her son's dark head.

"Christian tells me you have a daughter," she said, smiling up at Alex.

Alex nodded and glowed with maternal pride. "Isabella. She's ten months old."

"We'll have to get together some evening. I can warn you all about the terrible twos."

"Splendid idea!" Christian beamed, seizing the opportunity with gusto. "Why don't we do it over dinner? The four of us at Nick's."

Maggie gave him a look. "Maybe when Alex isn't so busy," she said pointedly. "She's going to be exhausted, what with having to do your riding on top of her own."

Christian frowned at her. Loyalty to gender. He should have expected as much. He shifted on his crutches, guilt nipping at him.

Guilt! Gads, he never felt guilt! It wasn't as if Alex was doing his riding for free. And it wasn't as if he weren't really hurt. Besides, Alex needed to become acquainted with the caliber of horse she deserved. She belonged on mounts like Diamond Life and Legendary, not Terminator. He was doing this for her own good. He all but told her as much a few minutes later, after Maggie had said her good-byes and led Buddy away toward the house.

He invited Alex into the dispensary, where the

communal coffee pot was kept. Setting his crutches aside so he could use his hands, he poured two cups and offered one to Alex. They leaned back against the counter and discussed the way the stallion had gone and what the training strategy was to have him ready for the upcoming show. Eventually Christian managed to turn the conversation Alex's way.

"You're really very talented, Alex," he said. "And that isn't simple flattery. Any number of top stables would be lucky to have you, and I think you know it."

Oh, I know it, Alex thought, glancing away. She also knew that no top stable would hire her without proper references, and her last employer would hardly write a glowing recommendation. By the time the Reidells got through running her down, she'd be lucky to get a job mucking out stalls at a sale barn.

"Why are you doing this, Alex?" Christian asked, bemused. "Why put up with bastards like Haskell and Terminator when you don't have to?"

"I want to be my own boss," she answered truthfully enough, though she still avoided his eyes. "I put up with Tully and Terminator because that's what I have to do if I want to ride A Touch of Dutch. They're a package deal."

"You don't need rides that badly."

She lifted a black brow but kept her temper in check, projecting ice instead of fire. "Who are you to say so?"

Christian slammed his coffee mug down as an irrational burst of responsibility surged through him. "Dammit, Alex, I'll send you some of my own if that's what it takes. I can't stand to see you risking your neck on that rogue."

"It's my neck," she said stubbornly.

Christian heaved a sigh as he watched her chin go up. "There goes the drawbridge," he muttered.

Alex gave him a suspicious look. "What?"

"Nothing." He shook his head wearily, his shoulders slumping. He ran a hand back through his pale hair and sighed again. "You're right, of course, it's none of my business. Forgive me for being indiscriminately concerned. I really don't know what's gotten into me lately."

Join the club, Alex thought as she stared pensively into her coffee. She had come to Virginia with a simple outline for her life. Suddenly things were getting complicated beyond belief. She found herself recklessly drawn to a man who had a reputation for collecting hearts like charms for a bracelet. She found herself liking him, wanting to be with him, yearning for another of his kisses.

It was the height of folly. Even if she let herself think there could be something special between her and Christian Atherton, even if she agreed to go out with him, what would ultimately come of it? He would expect things to progress on their natural course. What would Christian think of her when she finally told him about her past, which she would have to do. It wouldn't be fair not to tell him. Would he believe her side of the story when no one else had—including her own family? Why would he, she wondered cynically.

"Where do you go?" Christian asked on a whisper, his eyes as deep and blue as the sea as he leaned nearer. "Where do you go when you drift away?"

"Nowhere," Alex murmured, knowing the lie was plain on her face.

The corner of Christian's mouth tilted up. "You're such a mystery."

"No, I'm not!" she insisted too vehemently, instinctively wary of having him want to solve the puzzle. She suddenly remembered seeing a shelf full of mystery novels in his cottage, and her blood ran cold. She actually felt herself go pale. "There's nothing mysterious about me! I'm just trying to make a life as best I can."

"All right, all right," Christian murmured, calming her with his soothing, mesmerizing voice. He lifted a hand to gently brush her hair out of her eyes. "It's all right."

Alex relaxed by degrees, her breath gradually coming in slower gasps.

"It's all right," Christian whispered again, inching closer.

He stroked her cheek, running his thumb along her jaw and tilting her head back with subtle pressure. Their gazes locked, and for an instant there was a communication flowing between them that defied words, a current of feeling that was strong and undeniable. Then his lashes fluttered down as he slowly lowered his mouth to hers.

Alex drank in his kiss with a sense of desperation as emotions tore loose from their moorings inside her and crashed into one another. She wanted him, she wanted no one. She wanted to feel, she wanted to remain numb. She wanted a life without memories, she could never forget.

Passion won out momentarily as she blocked out the maelstrom of other emotions. For just an instant she let herself respond the way a woman would want to respond with a handsome, charming man kissing her—hungrily.

Christian groaned low in his throat. Gently he pinned Alex against the counter, flanking her legs with his own. He ran a hand over her short hair, down the sleek column of her throat, down to cup her small, full breast through the loose black polo shirt she wore, and groaned again as her nipple budded beneath his thumb.

"Oh, Alex," he said, his voice low and hoarse, tortured and ecstatic.

He wanted her with a fierceness he hadn't experienced since his youth. Just one touch, one taste, and he was hard and straining against the fly of his jeans. He tilted his hips into hers, letting her feel what she was doing to him, letting her know in no uncertain terms what he wanted. Just the thought of her tight, hot warmth closing around him bumped his pulse up another notch. The idea of having her naked and willing in his arms sent heat flaming through him.

He kissed her again, this time seeking entrance to her mouth and all the warm, honeyed delights he knew he would find there. Alex sagged against him for just a second or two, giving in to what she had forbidden herself—the comfort of being held, the electricity of desire, the building sense of urgency.

Feelings she had denied for so long rushed to the surface with overwhelming force, and panic was not far behind. She pulled away from him quickly, almost frantically.

"No," she said in a tortured whisper as old feelings of guilt and shame swirled with disappointment and despair inside her. She pushed Christian back with her palms splayed across his chest. She couldn't bring herself to look up at him, afraid of what she might see in his eyes. She focused instead on her fingers and the royal blue jersey beneath them.

"Alex?" Christian asked, stunned by her sudden change of heart. She had been responding so sweetly, her body arching into his, her mouth wild and sweet.

"No," she mumbled again, tears choking her as she stumbled for the door. She pulled up in the doorway, fighting her own urge to flee. Chest heaving, she swallowed hard and said, "I . . . have to get back to work."

Christian watched her go, utterly confused and utterly frustrated. He wasn't used to having a lady fight off the pleasant temptation of desire. Why had Alex? She was single, unattached, definitely attracted to him. There was no earthly reason why they shouldn't simply enjoy the mutual magnetism. And yet there had been the unmistakable bleak look of self-recrimination in her expression before she'd turned and run.

He had a strong urge to go after her, but he fought it. She obviously wanted time alone. He would give her the chance to sort out her feelings. Going back to the cupboard, he poured himself another cup of coffee and drank it as he mused about the whirlwind of a woman's emotions.

Ry stomped into the dispensary, grumbling. "Can you believe that Tully Haskell? Called to try to sell me that daughter of Abdullah when he knows damn well she isn't sound. As if I'd ever buy anything from him." He poured himself a cup of coffee and jabbed his friend with a pointed look. "I wouldn't buy a talking dog from Tully Haskell for a nickel, if it sat right up and called me sweetheart. What's the matter with you?"

Nothing Alex Gianni couldn't fix in the course of a long, hot night, Christian thought ruefully. "Nothing," he said. "Just pondering the fact that women are impossible to figure out."

"Well, hell," Ry growled. "I could have told you that."

Six

Alex leaned against the dun mare's side, her eyes drifting shut as sleep beckoned. For the fifth day she had risen at five A.M. to see to some of her own chores before leaving to ride Christian's horses. She would be home by noon, grab a quick bite, and play with Isabella for a few minutes. Then it would be back in the saddle, riding her own string of six horses in training. Then came after-school riding lessons for three students, evening chores, supper, Isabella's bath and bedtime, another hour in the barn to tend to the mare's injured foot, book work until she dozed off, a few hours' fitful sleep, and the process would start all over again.

Charlie had been a big help with chores and grooming. She would have been an even bigger help if Alex would have allowed it. But Alex was determined not to become dependent on having a stable hand. It was her place, not Christian Atherton's. The idea of accepting help from him made her uncomfortable. Old instincts died hard. The one that told her men didn't do favors without expecting something in return prodded at her like a stone in her shoe.

She wanted to trust him. He deserved to have her trust him. Experience had bred caution in her, taught her not to give her trust so easily. She had learned to look for subtle signs of a person's trust-worthiness—the way his contemporaries related to him, the way his employees regarded him. Christian was widely liked by his peers. The people working for him respected him because he treated them well. There were no sidelong, furtive looks following him down the aisle after an order was given. By all signs large and small he was a good man. A tad too sure of himself and inclined to play the rake, but a good man where it counted.

Sighing, Alex bent to check the temperature of the water the horse was soaking its abscessed hoof in. She added a little from the steaming bucket she had carried down from the house and tossed in another handful of Epsom salts. The mare, a boarder's field hunter, dozed. Alex resumed her casual position against the horse's side and let her mind wander back over the past few days.

She had done her best to avoid Christian the remainder of her first day at Quaid Farm—not because she had been afraid of him, but because she had been ashamed of herself for letting something get started that she couldn't finish. It was best for both of them that they not exceed the bounds of friendship.

Guilt made a return visit now as she recalled how Christian had finally caught up with her as she'd been about to leave.

"Alex, I'm sorry."

"For what?"

The wind riffled that one roguish strand of hair that fell across his forehead, and he shrugged, a gesture that was the embodiment of male confusion. "Obviously, I upset you. . . ." He let the words trail off, at a loss for the reason.

Alex shook her head and stared down at the gravel of the drive.

"I'm the one who should apologize," she said. But the explanation didn't come. Like a logjam trying to move through the narrow neck of a river, the words and reasons stuck in her throat and built up until she could feel the pressure of them.

"I get very high marks for listening," he said

softly, his cultured voice as warm and comforting as flannel on a damp fall day.

Alex just sighed and shook her head again, slowly, regretfully. It was a story best left untold, for everyone's sake.

She repeated that to herself now as she leaned against the dun mare. It had become a litany in the last few days as Christian had done his best to charm her and she had done her best to resist him. A litany with dwindling conviction behind it. Conviction that ebbed during the course of long, lonely nights.

Her shoulders jumped and fell with her breath as she rested her cheek against the horse's side and closed her eyes. She was so tired. Physically tired. Tired of the sleepless nights. She had been born with emotions that ran high and close to the surface. She was tired from having to suppress them. Tired of altering herself into some pale, unnoticeable, inoffensive imitation of her former self, and afraid that in the end she would become someone even she didn't recognize.

"How are all my stars?"

The bellowing voice jolted Alex from her trance. She jerked awake with a gasp and a start, spooking the mare, who bolted, overturning the bucket. Tepid water sloshed out, soaking Alex's sneakers and washing across the cracked concrete floor of the barn's aisle in a dark stain.

"Didn't mean to startle you there, sweetheart," Tully Haskell said with a rather unconvincing gleam in his cold little eyes. He rolled a fat, inch-long stub of a cigar between his thumb and forefinger.

"Mr. Haskell," Alex said, automatically putting up the shield of cool control. She righted the bucket and set it aside. The dun mare stood at attention, but didn't show any signs of coming unglued. A good attitude to adopt, Alex decided. "What brings you out this way so early in the morning?"

"Does a man need an excuse to call on a pretty gal these days?"

Alex bit back the retort that was burning on her tongue. It seemed enough punishment for Tully that she did not respond to his sexist remark with a becoming blush and batting eyelashes. He frowned briefly, then ducked under the cross tie, coming close enough to make Alex want to step back.

"I'm out this way to check on a project. My company is building a two-hundred-fifty-thousand-dollar house on Valley Road, and I don't trust the lazy bastards on the crew to get it right." He jammed his cigar stub between his teeth, but it had gone out and acted only as an ugly accessory to his fleshy face. "You gotta stay on top of employees."

Gritting her teeth, Alex moved past him to unhook the horse from the cross ties. "I hope you don't mind if I work while we talk. I have to leave in a few minutes."

"You're working too hard for such a little gal. Ought to have a man around here, don't you think?"

She muttered a few words in Italian as she put the mare back in her stall.

"How's that?"

"Nothing," she answered, fairly certain he wouldn't want to hear that she thought his brain resided in a much lower region of his body than his head.

"Anyhow," Tully went on, never terribly concerned with what anyone else was thinking, "I just swung in to check with you about next weekend. You're taking the horses to Front Royal?"

"Yes. I'll be leaving early Saturday morning."

"And you're staying in what motel?"

"I'm . . . staying with an old girlfriend," she lied smoothly, her deep-seated sense of caution asserting itself. She let herself out of the stall and leaned against the door, staring in at the unremarkable mare because she didn't want to look at Tully. She disliked him intensely and wasn't all that sure of her ability to keep it out of her expression.

"Hmmm," Tully mused. "Well, fine." He planted a big hand on her shoulder and shot her a wink and a grin that was meant to bring a teasing quality to his next words. "I'll be there to give you a kiss in the winner's circle."

Alex barely suppressed the urge to gag at the thought. She gave him a pained smile and shot the bolt home in the mare's stall with unnecessary force. "I'll see you in Front Royal then, Mr.Haskell."

"You can count on that," Tully said.

As he moved away from her he let his hand trail down her back. Alex jumped a bit, sure she felt him pinch her bottom, but when she wheeled to glare accusingly at him, he was sauntering away without giving her a backward glance.

Swearing liberally, she snatched up the empty bucket and stormed into the tack room, banging it against the wall as she went in an effort to blow off some of her steam. She cursed herself out of habit and Tully out of simple dislike. Why had she attracted the likes of him? Why couldn't a dotty little old lady own A Touch of Dutch? She'd never been tempted to slap a little old lady. She'd never been nervous around little old ladies either.

And I won't be nervous around Haskell, she told herself, relaxing with an effort. She didn't have anything to worry about. She hadn't encouraged his advances. He wasn't likely to take them beyond the harmless flirtation stage.

Something scuffed the floor behind her, and she whirled with her heart in her throat, eyes wide, adrenaline pumping, instincts on red alert, only to find the source of her panic was the scruffy old barn cat. The bedraggled gray feline looked up at her, a freshly caught mouse drooping from its jaws. Then it turned and ran away, leaving Alex to lean weakly against the saddle rack, trying to put the memory that had shaken loose back into its sealed black box in her mind.

Christian steered his silver Mercedes carefully off the road and up the pitted, rutted stretch of gravel

Alex called a driveway. Once in the farmyard he parked near the barn, briefly contemplating ramming Charlie Simmonds's red-and-white motorbike where it leaned against the weathered side of the building. The only thing that saved him from doing it was the respect he had for his own vehicle and the distaste he had for facing Marcel, the Frenchman who serviced the machine at a specialty garage in Alexandria.

Charlie Simmonds was a blight on his life. He cursed the day her parents had met. It was because of Charlie he was feeling so guilty.

"Ought to be ashamed of yourself," she'd said, screwing her face into a scowl that made her little eyes all but disappear. "Working herself to a limp frazzle, poor little miss. And for what? So you can lay around on your ruddy bum and watch. Selfish, selfish. That's you all over. What a bloody crying shame it is. Better than the likes of you, that's what she deserves, all right, poor little miss."

Even now he growled at the thought of the dressing-down Charlie had given him the night before. She'd ridden up to the farm on her motorbike after evening chores for the sole purpose of giving him a tongue-lashing.

As a result he hadn't slept a wink and had instead spent the entire night berating himself for being a devious, selfish, uncaring cad. These were not welcome feelings, but he couldn't shake them. He couldn't even find any comfort in the knowledge that he had never denied being selfish, that what Charlie called devious tendencies he considered clever thinking, that by uncaring she meant self-absorbed, which he had never denied either. He was a confirmed bachelor, for heaven's sake! Those were all perfectly ordinary traits for a confirmed bachelor.

Grumbling under his breath, he climbed out of his sports car already dressed for riding in black breeches and a khaki polo shirt. His ankle was still sore, but it was nothing he hadn't endured before.

He merely ignored it as best he could as he walked into the poorly lit barn, limping slightly.

It wasn't entirely his fault Alex was overworked, he told himself for the millionth time. He'd sent her a groom, hadn't he? For all her cheek Charlie was a good worker. There was no reason Alex couldn't have been making better use of her, no reason Alex should have to get up an hour early to do tasks Charlie could easily handle.

Stubborn, that's what she was. Bloody stubborn. And a damned attractive trait it was. He ground his teeth at the thought. Where were these ludicrous ideas coming from? Full breasts were an attractive trait, not pigheadedness.

He turned in at the open tack-room door, alarm spurring his pulse into overdrive. Alex was bent over a saddle rack, her eyes squeezed tightly shut, her skin as pale as porcelain. He was across the small room in one stride.

"Alex!" He grabbed her upper arms, fearing she was ill or in pain. Certainly she looked weak.

Her eyes flew open, and the stark terror he saw there was like an electric jolt to his heart. In a purely instinctive reaction, she jerked back with enough force to pull him into the opposite side of the saddle rack.

"Alex, it's me!" he said, not realizing his fingers were biting into her flesh. He'd never had a woman look at him with such pure horror. It was a terrible feeling. "For God's sake, calm down!"

She stared at him for a tense moment as if she had no idea who he was. Then everything started to click into place. The fear left her eyes—but the general wariness didn't. Her body relaxed visibly, her shoulders sagging. She started breathing again, slowly and regularly.

"Christian," she said evenly. "You startled me."

"Startled you?" he said, incredulous, still shaken to the core. "Frightened to death is more like it. What's the matter? I came in and saw you bent over this saddle. . . ."

She looked down at the smooth dark leather, feeling she'd made a disastrous slip. He'd seen her with her guard completely down. It made her feel too vulnerable.

"Alex?"

"Nothing. I had a cramp, that's all."

She fully expected him to drop the topic. No man of her acquaintance had ever wanted to hear any of the gory details of a woman's life. It was a topic guaranteed to scare them off. But then, most men weren't Christian Atherton.

"You're lying," he said flatly, too upset to be polite. "Good Lord, Alexandra, you reacted as if you thought I was going to attack you!"

Instantly she dodged his gaze, glancing toward the open door, unwittingly answering a question that was only half-formed in his mind. The sudden knowledge was a worse shock than her response had been.

"Oh, my . . ." His voice trailed off, and his hands fell away from her as a nauseating weakness spread through him. Leaning back against the saddle rack behind him, he ran a hand back through his hair. He thought of every time she'd shied away from him, of the way she'd thrown him that first day when he'd startled her from behind. Finally it all made sense. Terrible sense.

Alex pressed back against the rough wood wall, wishing with all her heart she could melt right through it. The instant Christian had realized the truth, he had taken his hands off her, as if she were unclean, as if he hoped it wasn't too late to save himself from being tainted. But that was exactly what she had expected.

"Alex," he murmured, lifting his gaze to hers, anguish plain in the fathomless blue depths. "I'm so sorry. I had no idea."

What happened now? she wondered. Did they just say their good-byes and go their separate ways? Why hadn't he just stayed away from the beginning?

They would have both been spared the embarrassment of this moment.

"Do you want to tell me what happened?" Christian asked gently. She looked so alone, so uncomfortable, as if she would have crawled right out of her skin had that been an option. Her shoulders were squared, tensed, pressed back against the wall, her hands splayed against the rough pine boards. She looked like someone expecting a firing squad and no blindfold.

Alex supposed she could have escaped. She doubted Christian would come after her. But she was tired of running. It wasn't in her nature. Stand and fight had always been her motto. She had stood her ground and fought before and come away battered and bloody, disillusioned by everyone and everything she had ever believed in. The choice now was simple in her eyes. She had nothing left to lose.

"My last name was DeGrazia then," she began.

"Alexandra DeGrazia," Christian murmured, the puzzle piece falling into place. "I saw you ride in California." He stared down at the saddle in front of him as if he could see the whole scene on it. "A three-day event outside of Napa. I was there looking at a mare who showed promise in the show ring but not cross-country."

"My husband Michael and I were riding for Wide Acre Farm, the Reidells," she prompted.

"Yes," he said, but there was no further dawning of understanding.

He didn't know. How ironic, Alex thought, almost tempted to laugh. She had been so sure her married name would evoke gasps and looks of self-righteous reproach from everyone who heard it. Because she had been the one at the center of the storm, she had been certain every third person in the free world had known about the trial.

Somehow it would have been easier if Christian had known. He would have absorbed the details from the media and formed the same opinion everyone else had—that she was a liar. Now she would have the chance to tell her side once again. But no one else had ever believed her, so why would she think Christian might? Christian Atherton, of all people. A deep depression settled in her heart at the thought that he would leave her life now.

She sighed, conceding defeat, then told her tale in the flat, emotionless tone of a victim who has somehow managed to distance herself from the incident after being forced to relive it again and again.

"We had been working at Wide Acre about six months. It was going well. We got along well enough with Mr. Reidell. His son Greg was about our age, a little younger. I guess he was twenty-two or twenty-three, and I was twenty-five. We were friends—Greg and Michael, Greg and I. At least, I thought he was my friend. He was always making . . . remarks to me. Personal remarks. I thought he was teasing. I always gave him a sassy answer. One evening when Michael was gone, Greg came to our apartment and told me it was time I made good on all that talk. He raped me."

Christian felt the words like a physical blow. He hurt for Alex, for what she had been through. To force a woman was unthinkable to him, an intolerable act of violence. And the knowledge that Greg Reidell was handsome and educated and well-off made it all the more despicable.

"I pressed charges," Alex went on, condensing what had seemed an unending nightmare to the barest of facts. "But I didn't have any real proof. It was his word against mine, his family's money and power against a little nobody. He claimed I had been having an affair with him for months, that I liked it a little rough, which discounted the doctor's testimony. He claimed he told me he was going to break it off, and that I was just trying to get back at him, humiliate him, that I was angling for a big chunk of hush money since I couldn't sleep my way into the family. Of course, he was too virtuous to pay for something he hadn't done, so he let the case come to trial to reveal me for the lying, conniving slut I was."

"The bastard," Christian muttered, his voice trembling with fury. His hands clenched into fists at his side, and for the first time in his life he knew what it was to want to kill another human being. "The bloody bastard."

Alex looked up at him with a strange, bemused expression. "You believe me?" she said incredulously.

Christian's brows pulled together, and he frowned at her. "Of course I believe you. Why wouldn't I believe you?"

"Because no one else did," she said simply.

"You mean, no one outside your family."

"I mean no one."

Her family had offered minimal token support. They had taken her in after her marriage had crumbled, but they hadn't been doing her a favor. It had been an obligation. The Gianni men had been inclined to loyalty toward their gender. The Gianni women had been full of reproach about the way she flirted, the way she dressed, the profession she pursued. All of them had been vaguely ashamed. None of them had believed Greg Reidell would have forced a woman. He was too handsome, too wealthy. He didn't fit their idea of a rapist, and they weren't inclined to change their preconceived ideas—because then their neatly ordered world would be in danger of tilting on its axis. If a man like Greg Reidell could be capable of rape, then who were they supposed to trust, what were they supposed to believe in?

Their subtle betrayal hadn't made her angry, just sad. It had made her see them as ordinary, flawed humans. The idyllic family of her memories had ceased to exist.

"Surely, your husband . . ." Christian said, looking helpless.

Alex smiled sadly. "Michael tried, but he felt betrayed and he felt guilty, and in the end he just couldn't deal with it. He was always the jealous type. Reidell's lies played on that, preyed on his mind."

She sighed and combed a hand back through her

bangs. "I was pregnant with Isabella when it happened. Just a month or so along. I hadn't told Michael yet. I was waiting for the right time," she said with an ironic twist to her mouth. "When I did tell him, he wouldn't believe me when I said the baby couldn't be Greg's. I think that was what ultimately ended the marriage. He couldn't bear the thought of raising another man's child."

As her words trailed off into the silence of the tack room, Alex let the last of the tension drain from her muscles. She was so tired, tired of running from who she was, tired of the fear of ridicule, of the speculative looks. She wished Christian would just leave so she could curl up in a corner and shut the world out with sleep.

Christian studied her quietly. He remembered again the laughing, lovely girl he'd seen in California, so full of spirit and youthful innocence, and he mourned her loss. Now he took in the cropped hair, the drab, baggy sweatshirt, the world-weary eyes, and the dark shadows beneath them—the disguise of a woman haunted by her past. And everything inside him ached for her. She'd been so alone. She'd been doubted by the people she had needed most. Now he understood her obsessive self-reliance. Now he understood a lot of things.

Protectiveness, possessiveness, sifted through him. He was so absolutely focused on Alex, though, that he didn't try to escape them this time. For perhaps the first time in his life his own needs had become secondary.

"I'd take it all away if I could," he whispered, stepping forward and gathering her in his arms. He pulled her close and pressed a kiss to her temple.

Alex pressed her cheek to his chest, stunned for an instant. She had become so used to the rejection, the doubts. But there were no doubts from Christian. He was holding her the way she had longed to be held, giving her the human contact she had been denied. The people she had loved had treated her like a leper, and this man she barely knew was holding her and sharing her pain and offering his comfort.

For the first time in forever she allowed the tears to fall. They streamed down her cheeks and soaked into the soft cotton of Christian's knit shirt. All the hurt and the loneliness poured out, leaving her empty and exhausted.

When the river of tears had finally ceased to flow, Christian gallantly handed her a handkerchief dug out of the small zippered pocket of his breeches. Then he bent and swept her up into his arms and started for the door.

"What are you doing?" Alex asked, her voice hoarse from crying. She swiped at the moisture still clinging to her lashes and let out a little yelp as Christian hefted her slight weight in his arms, resettling her. "Put me down," she demanded weakly even as her arms slid willingly around his neck.

"I'm taking you to the house," he said firmly. His expression brooked no disobedience. "You're taking the day off to rest. Look the word up in the dictionary if you need to."

"But I have work to do!"

"I'll ride your horses for you."

"But—"

He gave her a fierce, hawkish look. "No arguments."

"But your ankle—"

"Is well enough. I'll manage."

Alex opened her mouth again but snapped it shut as Christian arched a brow in warning. She felt a ridiculously strong urge to giggle. In fact, she felt euphoric.

They went in the kitchen door just as Charlie was coming out dragging her jacket in one hand. Alex ducked to hide her tearstained face against Christian's neck, breathing in his warm, clean male scent.

"Blimey, Miss Alex, are you hurt?" the girl asked anxiously, dancing around them like a fractious beagle, her earrings clanging together.

"Nnnnn . . ." Alex muttered, shaking her head against Christian's throat.

"She's not injured," Christian insisted, trying to brush past the concerned, curious groom. "I simply wanted to carry her."

"Gosh, gov, that's a bit Stone Age, isn't it?" Charlie teased, dark eyes crinkling as she stepped back.

Christian scowled at her. "Go mousse your hair or something, Simmonds."

Charlie sniffed in mock affront. "Go on. There's work to be done. Something you wouldn't know anything about."

She sauntered off toward the barn, whistling, her rubber chore boots scuffing on the gravel drive.

In the kitchen Christian deposited Alex on an old chrome-and-red vinyl chair and turned to Pearl, who was busy at the stove.

"Pearl, see that Alex eats an enormous breakfast and goes straight to bed."

Pearl stared at him, spatula in hand. "Have you lost your mind or something, Mr. Atherton?"

Or something, Christian thought, looking down at Alex, who now held Isabella in her lap. The first tremors of fear shuddered through him. Alex was staring up at him, her amber eyes still wet with tears. A soft smile curved her lush mouth. Isabella looked up at him as well, her eyes dark brown and sparkling with wonder. They made a lovely picture— a family, minus one.

Christian's throat constricted. A chill raced over him. He backed toward the door.

"I'll check in on you later," he said, then let himself out into the fresh morning air without waiting for a reply of any kind.

"Good Lord," he muttered as he wandered away from the house. "I feel weak and hot and cold and rather ill in general. And I'm talking to myself." He stopped in his tracks, going pale as his eyes widened in the horror of sudden realization.

He was in love!

In love. Gads! He had never meant to fall in love.

Love was serious stuff. Love meant responsibility for another person. In his case it meant taking responsibility not only for a lady with a wealth of hurt in her past but with a baby as well. A baby! The very thought made him shudder clear down to his boots.

He closed his eyes and was immediately confronted with the image of Alex and Isabella gazing up at him. His heart melted like butter in his chest. He was well and truly in love. Christian Atherton, heartthrob of the show-jumping set, playboy extraordinaire, was irretrievably in love with an amber-eyed minx and her darling daughter. How the mighty bachelor had fallen.

The question was: Could he get Alex to fall as well? Would he be able to bridge the hurt others had caused her and win not only her trust but her heart in the bargain?

The determination and competitive nature that had taken him to the top of his profession surged to the forefront, bringing with it strength. He straightened his elegant shoulders and lifted his aristocratic chin.

He'd had princesses eating out of his hand. He'd had some of the most wealthy, powerful women in the world beg for his affection. Could he get Alexandra Gianni to fall in love with him? Bloody well right he could!

Seven

"Here comes another one, Alex!" Charlie called from the open end of the barn. She stood with a shoulder braced lazily against the door frame, watching as the blue-and-gray pickup from Quaid Farm bounced its way up the drive. "What do you suppose he's sent this time?"

"I can't imagine." Alex stepped out of the tack room and around her daughter's walker.

"No, no, Mama!" Isabella squealed and stormed down the aisle after her, chubby arms waving, walker wheels chattering on the concrete. She chanted her favorite new words incessantly, making them into a song of sorts. "No, no, no, no, mine! Mine, mine, mine!"

"He sends any more flowers, an' you'll be able to open a bloomin' green'ouse." Charlie slapped her skinny thigh and laughed at her own joke, her eyes squinting into slits.

Alex smiled and wiped the saddle soap off her hands and onto her breeches. In the two weeks that had passed since she had made her confession to Christian, he had done anything but shrink away from her. He had been even more determined in his courtship. He sent her a present every day—a single rose, a bunch of balloons, a clutch of violets. The ones he delivered in person were accompanied by delicious kisses Alex no longer tried to fend off.

Not above bribing a baby, Christian had brought Isabella little trinkets as well and had already completely won over the littlest Gianni. Isabella had gotten to the point where she brightened into unrestrained excitement every time she saw Christian. A sneaky tactic, Alex thought, but an effective one. The way to a mother's heart was through her baby. The sight of the elegant Mr. Atherton, the galloping playboy, playing with a baby—and thoroughly enjoying it—was downright impossible to resist.

Thanks to Christian's wooing, Alex found her heart cautiously considering coming out of its shell. Christian Atherton was a wonderful man—charming, sweet, fun to be with. He had brightened her days immeasurably. He had shown her there was a lot more to him than an attractive exterior and a rakish reputation.

They had fought tooth and nail over the issue of Charlie staying on, even though Alex was no longer riding at Quaid Farm. After revealing her past, Alex's instinct had been to retreat. As soon as she had recovered from a giddy sense of relief once things were in the open, her old caution had returned. She was determined to make her way, to pay her own bills, to accept favors from no one.

Christian had been unshakable, however. He had insisted Alex keep his cockney charge, claiming that only a fool would turn down free help. Alex had relented, albeit reluctantly. She might have been many things, but she had ceased to be a fool some time ago. Finally, she had given in.

Christian had rewarded her with another of his mind-numbing kisses. Residual heat seeped through her at the memory of it. The man had world-class lips. He hadn't pressed her for a more physical relationship, but he had made it clear that when she was ready, he would be more than willing.

The idea both frightened and excited her. It had been a long time since she'd been with a man. She and Michael had never made love after the rape. He hadn't wanted to, and she hadn't pressed him, because she'd been afraid of how she would react, afraid of the possibility that she might not be able to enjoy it or that she might freeze up. In the end she had never had the chance to find out. Her husband had rejected her, unable to bear the thought that she'd been with another man. But Christian was showing no such prejudices. He didn't blame her for what had happened, nor did he view her as damaged goods.

Maybe it was time to try another relationship. She had come to Virginia to start a new life. There was no reason going out with Christian couldn't be a part of it. He certainly wasn't showing any signs of giving up on the idea, Alex thought with a wry smile as the Quaid Farm groom climbed out of the truck with a large brown cardboard box in his hands.

"Mornin', Ms. Gianni," he drawled with a shy grin. "Got somethin' for you from Mr. Atherton."

"She don't want it if it ain't a fur coat, ducky," Charlie teased, batting her spiky lashes at the gangly young groom. He blushed to the roots of his wheat-colored hair and grinned.

Alex took the box, her mouth dropping open in delighted surprise. "It's not just a fur coat, Charlie. It's five fur coats."

"Blimey!" Charlie exclaimed, abruptly breaking off from her flirting to wheel toward Alex and the box.

Five kittens, each with a blue bow tied around its neck, clambered over one another to get to the edge of the box so they could peer over the side. There was a gray-striped one, an orange-striped one, one that was black and white, one that was black and orange, and one calico. All of them were eager to get out and explore their new home.

Alex put the box down on the concrete, immediately gaining her daughter's wide-eyed attention. "Look, Isabella, kitties."

"Tees!" the baby said, bouncing in the seat of her walker. She banged a fist excitedly against the plastic tray as the kittens bounded out of the box. The little girl hurried down the aisle after them, laughing and jabbering. "No, no, tees!"

Alex watched them go, hugging herself as her heart warmed her from the inside out.

"Ma'am? Mr. Atherton said he'd stop by around dinner time," the groom said.

Alex thanked him, Charlie winked at him and told him to come back anytime. The groom blushed, tipped the brim of his battered baseball cap, and ambled away.

"What do you think of Christian, Charlie?" Alex asked absently, turning back to keep an eye on her daughter.

Charlie snorted and waved a hand with black polished fingernails and too many rings. "He's a stuffy, pompous, bossy bugger." Her mischievous smile spread across her face. "And you'd be barmy if you let him get away, a dishy guy like that."

"Yeah," Alex said on a sigh, her eyes sparkling as she watched Isabella play hide-and-seek with the kittens. "Maybe you're right."

Christian walked into Nick's Restaurant and was greeted immediately by the delicious aroma of simmering tomatoes and herbs. The restaurant didn't officially open for business until eleven A.M., but he had a great deal to do before he could put his plan into motion, and he knew Nick would already be hard at work in the kitchen.

He strolled through the main dining room, admiring the antiques and the masculine decor. Maggie Quaid and Nick's wife Katie—who was also Rylan Quaid's baby sister—had done the decorating, choosing a soothing color scheme of rich dark green and warm beige. The restaurant was housed in a two-hundred-year-old building that had once been a menswear store, and leftover treasures of that time adorned the walls—bowlers and walking sticks and displays of shirt collars. The overall effect was welcoming and comfortable. The restaurant had quickly become one of the most popular in the Briarwood area.

The sight that he saw as he pushed through the kitchen door brought a smile to Christian's lips. Nick Leone had his petite wife in a passionate embrace and was kissing her thoroughly. Neither of them noticed the intrusion, so engrossed were they in expressing their feelings for each other. They looked as if they should have been posing for the cover of a romantic novel. Nick was big and muscular. His black hair tumbled across his forehead. He banded his arms around Katie's slender frame, almost lifting her off the ground. Katie's fall of silky, waist-long chestnut hair flowed behind her.

Christian cleared his throat discreetly.

"We don't open yet," Nick growled in a thick New Jersey accent, his attention still solely on his wife.

Katie, however, turned toward him, her gray eyes glowing, cheeks blooming a becoming shade of pink to match the piping on her Laura Ashley dress. "Hi, Christian. What brings you to town in the middle of the morning?"

"An errand *de amour*," he said, smiling.

"Ah, *amore*!" Nick grinned, the interruption instantly forgotten. "Who's the lucky lady? Anyone we know?"

"I don't think so. She's new to the area. Alexandra Gianni."

Nick was visibly pleased. "A good Italian girl." He nodded sagely. "That's just what you need—a good Italian girl to make an honest man of you." He slapped Christian on the shoulder, his dark eyes gleaming with good humor. "And if she can't do it, her brothers will."

"What if she hasn't any brothers?"

He waved the notion away. "She's Italian. Trust me. She's got brothers, she's got uncles, she's got cousins. At the very least, she's got a godfather."

Christian lifted a blond brow, his mouth twitching with amusement. "Like in the movies?"

Nick laughed and shook a finger at him. "You better hope not."

"Maggie tells me this could be something special,"

Katie said with feminine relish for all things romantic. "What can we do to help?"

Lifting the wicker basket he'd borrowed from Maggie, Christian grinned engagingly. "Fit me out with your finest picnic lunch for two."

"I can't believe I'm doing this," Alex said half to herself.

She twirled the stem of the tulip-shaped glass between her fingers, watching the sunlight play through the white wine. On the red-and-white checkered cloth beneath her were white china plates strewn with the remnants of a marvelous meal—cold breast of chicken oreganato, tortellini salad, fresh Italian bread with herb butter, two kinds of cheese and grapes. She felt pleasantly stuffed and sleepy as the strengthening spring sun shone down on them.

"I should be working," she murmured with a minimum of conviction, shifting her position so she was lying back on her elbows. She turned her face to the sun and sighed.

"You know what they say about all work," Christian said, regarding her over the rim of his own wineglass.

"Yes. It pays my rent."

"Even you need to break for lunch, darling. We must eat, so why not eat the finest?"

That was Christian's life philosophy in a nutshell, Alex thought with a wry smile. Driving was necessary, so why not own a Mercedes? Clothing was necessary, so why not buy designer labels? He was an aristocrat through and through, but there was something sweet about his inborn snobbishness. It was never too serious or malicious, more of a front than anything, a shield to hide the sensitive inner man.

"Your friend is a wonderful cook."

"Yes, he is, and he insists we join him and his wife for dinner one evening very soon," Christian said, never passing up an opportunity to ask Alex for a date. One of these days she was going to say yes.

Alex stared at him for a long moment, her amber eyes dark with drowsiness and contemplation. At length she nodded slowly and said, "I'd like that."

Christian nearly spilled his wine. "You would?"

"We must eat," she said, mimicking him. "Why not enjoy pleasant company while we do it?"

Christian felt his smile grow to idiotic proportions. "Why not, indeed."

They were passing a critical point in their relationship. He knew Alex was aware of it. He also knew she didn't want to call too much attention to it. She dodged his gaze almost shyly and played some more with her glass.

Lord, she's pretty, he thought, his heart swelling with the love he was slowly growing accustomed to. He let his eyes drink in the sight of her—the sophisticated cut of her dark hair, the delicate lines of her face with its perfectly feminine features. She had traded her breeches for an old pair of jeans with holes in the knees, and her boots for a disreputable looking pair of white canvas sneakers. She had changed out of the baggy black T-shirt she'd worn riding for an equally baggy olive polo shirt, but as she set her glass aside and leaned back on her hands, the outline of her small, full breasts was clearly visible.

There was certainly nothing fancy in the way she looked, he reflected. She wasn't wearing a trace of makeup. No cloud of expensive perfume surrounded her. She was dressed like a stable hand. He had dated women renowned for their striking beauty, women who wore one-of-a-kind gowns and jewelry to make a thief swoon with envy. Women with fortunes and women with power. But he had never felt about any of them the way he felt about Alex Gianni.

It was powerful and wonderful and terrifying. Fear seized him at the thought that she might not return the feelings or that she might return them with regrets. He felt like a right proper fool most of the time. And he wouldn't have traded it for anything.

Gads, I'm sunk, he thought with a rueful smile as he stretched out on his belly, never taking his eyes off Alex. What would Uncle Dicky say?

"This is much nicer than the last time we were here," Alex said.

Christian laughed. "I dare say."

They were in the high meadow where Christian had been injured trying to rescue her. The woods all around them was in full bloom, and wildflowers dotted the grass.

Christian had shown up, picnic basket in tow. He autocratically ordered Charlie to see to Isabella's every need as Pearl was gone for the day and then badgered Alex into eating with him. She was glad that she had come. Now that she'd settled a few things in her heart, it seemed right to spend a lazy spring afternoon with him.

Something warm and wonderful stirred inside her as she looked at him, at his handsome profile, the elegant way his sapphire blue knit shirt clung to his strong shoulders. He wore jeans and sneakers, but even in casual dress he exuded a sense of privilege and breeding. Alex decided it wouldn't have mattered how he dressed. The power of his personality blazed as strong and hot as the sun. It was the inner man, not his outer trappings, that drew her. She knew better than most that privilege and power didn't make a man superior. It was what was in his heart that counted. It was what she hoped was in Christian's heart that mattered to Alex.

She packed their dishes away while he watched her.

"You're very quiet," he commented, sitting up and draping one arm across a drawn-up knee.

"Mmmm . . . just thinking . . ."

"What about?"

Alex swallowed the fist-sized knot in her throat. "Us."

He straightened subtly. His eyes never left her face. "What about us?"

Lips pursed, she gave a little shrug that made her look very Italian. She busied her hands fussing with the picnic basket. "I just wondered . . . where we go from here."

Christian reached out to set the basket beyond her reach, then hooked a finger under her chin and tilted her face up so she had to meet his gaze. The intensity in her tawny eyes brought out the flecks of gold in the iris, dazzling him, but not quite hiding the wariness from him. Again he cursed the man who had put that look there, and again he vowed to do whatever was necessary to erase it. He wanted Alex so badly, he sometimes thought he wouldn't be able to endure the wait. But wait he would. He had no intention of rushing her into anything.

"That's entirely up to you, sweetheart," he murmured. "I'll do whatever you like."

"Will you?" Alex asked softly, afraid at how badly she needed to believe in him. If he let her down . . . If she let him down . . .

"Tell me what you want," he murmured. "I'll give you anything, Alex."

He couldn't give her back her past or her belief in the greater good of humankind, but he could give her a future, and he could give her his love. That was what shone in the blue of his eyes as he stared down at her, holding his breath, waiting for her answer.

Alex lifted a hand to brush her fingertips along the lean line of his cheek, as if she didn't quite believe he was real. "Will you make love to me?" she asked, her voice as soft as the wings of butterflies that skimmed over the green meadow, as soft as the breeze that brought the rich scents of the Virginia countryside.

"No," Christian whispered, taking her hand in his. "But I'll make love *with* you. I'll gladly make love *with* you, Alexandra."

Lifting her hand to his mouth, he pressed a kiss to each of her knuckles, never taking his eyes from hers. She watched him, her own eyes darkening with passion, her lips parting slightly.

"Are you afraid of me, Alex?" he asked.

She shook her head slowly. "No." A tiny smile twitched up one corner of her mouth. "I'm afraid of me."

"I'm not afraid of you."

To prove it he brought both her hands to his chest and abandoned them there in invitation. Alex screwed up her courage and reached back in her mind, past fear of rejection, past the horror of what had happened to her, back to when it had been all right to want and to please. She slid her palms down the solid wall of his chest, across his flat, hard belly to the waist of his jeans, and dragged his shirttail out. Then she reversed the process, letting her fingers explore the smooth contours of his body as she raised the hem of his shirt.

Christian discarded the garment, tossing it aside carelessly. His own gaze still locked on Alex, he let her look her fill as the sun beat down on the well-defined muscles of his shoulders, arms, and back. Years of demanding physical work had toned his sleek body to perfection. Alex caressed every smooth, hard plane, every mark of delineation. When she ceased her exploration, it was only to take Christian's hand and draw it to the hem of her shirt.

He undressed her slowly, checking his own rampant desire in favor of building her own. What he revealed was the embodiment of femininity. She was dainty and delicate, and she brought out every possessive instinct he had buried beneath his layers of sophistication. Her breasts were small but full, fitting perfectly into his hands, with pouting, dusky pink nipples that tightened at the touch of the breeze. Ever so gently he drew the pads of his thumbs across the turgid tips and groaned appreciatively as they rose to attention.

Alex sighed and let her head fall back and her eyes

drift shut. It felt so good to be touched, touched with reverence and care and sweet longing. She leaned back and drank in the sensation as Christian's gentle hands cupped her and caressed her. He blocked out the sun as he leaned down to kiss her, but Alex felt filled with golden light. She wrapped her arms around his neck and opened her mouth beneath his, inviting the intimacy she had so long been denied. His tongue slid along hers, velvety warm, stroking and retreating. And heat swirled through her, chasing out all the cold shadows of the past.

Never breaking the kiss, Christian rose slowly to his feet, lifting Alex with him. Simultaneously each found the button on the other's jeans and popped them free. Zippers rasped in a descending duet. Denim dropped to the checked cloth at their feet.

With trembling hands Alex lowered Christian's snug black briefs, freeing his manhood to her touch. He was smooth and hard, hot and ready, and the stunning sense of need that burned inside her as she stroked him filled her with a dizzying sense of relief. She pressed herself against him, kissing his chest, flicking her tongue over his flat male nipples, all the while rubbing and stroking the essence of what made him male.

Christian groaned at the exquisite torture. Desire doubled and tripled its hold on him as Alex's hold tormented him. He dragged her plain cotton panties down, splaying his hands over the soft fullness of her tight, well-rounded buttocks. He lifted her against him again so that she had to wrap her arms around his neck. His mouth took hers hungrily as her body arched into his, the downy thatch of curls at the apex of her thighs brushing sensually against his belly.

Slowly he lowered them both to the ground, settling Alex on her back and himself on his side next to her. He set off on an exploration of her body with his hands and lips that was meant to be unhurried. It was meant to slowly stoke the fire in both of them, to slowly bring the level of desire to a fever pitch. But Christian was already bordering on delirium. All the smooth, calm, thorough technique he had honed over the years deserted him. With Alex he knew an almost frantic urge to make her his, to purge every other man from her mind and stake his claim in the most basic way he could.

Struggling with the inner battle, he forced himself to slow the pace, knowing he wouldn't be able to stand it much longer, but fearing he would be rushing Alex if he gave in to his own needs. Gently he swept his hand down across her belly to the slick satin heat between her thighs. Kissing her deeply, he parted the delicate petals and eased a finger into the tight pocket of her womanhood, wringing a moan of unmistakable pleasure from her. Her hips pushed off the blanket, urging him, begging him until she was gasping for air.

"Christian, please," she whispered, clutching at his shoulders and trying to pull him onto her. "I need you. Please don't make me wait."

"Anything you ask, darling," he murmured, pulling away from her for the brief instant it took to dig into the hip pocket of his discarded jeans and pull out the familiar foil packet he'd tucked there in hope.

Alex stared up at him as he positioned himself above her, and felt a quick stab of apprehension. She didn't want to disappoint him. She didn't want to be disappointed. She wanted this to end as beautifully as it had progressed so far.

Christian leaned over her with a gentle smile and brushed her hair back. There was only one thing he could think to say that would allay her fears. He'd said it countless hundreds of times to more women than he cared to remember. But this time when he said it, it wasn't casual, and it came straight from his heart.

"I love you, Alex."

She succeeded in pulling him down to her then and lifted her hips to take him inside her. He filled her slowly, carefully, and when he was embedded deep within her, he checked to make sure she was all right, that she wasn't afraid or hurt. She was incredibly hot and tight around him, and his control was slipping through his grasp like a wet rope, but Alex's needs were uppermost in his mind.

"Oh, Christian." She sighed, her mouth curving into the most sensual of smiles beneath his. *"Tante grazie."*

She arched against him, savoring the feel of him inside her, celebrating the joy and the relief that washed through her. There were no dark memories, only pleasure—wondrous, exquisite pleasure. She felt new and whole and powerfully feminine. It was a feeling more intoxicating than the wine they'd shared.

"I only want to please you, Alex," Christian murmured, every word a kiss as he eased back and slowly moved into her again.

His muscles trembled with the effort to hold back. Alex moved beneath him, inviting him, luring him toward the edge of sexual bliss. Her small hands stroked down the arch of his back to his hips to knead his tight buttocks, to pull him even deeper into her heat.

"I want to take you to paradise, darling," he whispered, kissing her earlobe, tracing the shell of her ear with the tip of his tongue. He drove his hips against her again, slowly, strongly, stroking her in a way he knew would wring a startled gasp of pleasure from her.

Moaning, Alex breathed a stream of reverent Italian. Her nails raked down Christian's back as she murmured, "Paradise . . . let's go there together."

They moved in unison, both their bodies betraying a wonderful kind of urgency, until they were straining into each other, panting and smiling and, finally, replete.

Alex was so happy, she never wanted to move from the spot. She thought she could have stayed forever under the warm spring sun with bees buzzing lazily in the distance and Christian in her arms. But she knew there were horses waiting to be ridden, including Terminator, who had won his class the past Sunday, then proceeded to spend the week trying to throw her. He had succeeded once, flinging her headlong into the bars.

After a while she sat up and began to dress, pulling her shirt on over her head and handing Christian's to him. They kissed and giggled like teenagers as they put themselves back together. Alex found the torn foil wrapper and arched a brow.

"Always prepared?"

Christian flashed her his brilliant grin. "A useful motto I picked up in the Boy Scouts."

Alex shoved him playfully. "You liar. You were never a Boy Scout."

"I most certainly was," he insisted, lifting his square chin. "Until that camping incident with the Girl Guides, which got me chucked out."

"You're too much." Alex groaned, rolling her eyes as she reached for her panties.

"That's not what you were saying a moment ago," Christian murmured in a dark velvet voice as he pulled her against him.

The gold in Alex's eyes glittered like pyrite as she snuggled into him. "Wicked."

"Thoroughly."

He leaned down to kiss her, but something on her hip caught his eye, and he pulled back suddenly with a scowl as black as a thundercloud. "What the bloody hell is that?"

Alex's gaze flicked down over her right hip. The bruise was three days old, just turning a truly putrid shade of green. It was a good five inches across, and while it looked horrible, it marked only a small area of what actually hurt. As bumps and bruises were typical in her line of work, she had ignored it. Nothing was broken, that was all that really mattered.

Christian was standing in front of her with his hands planted at the waist of his jeans, his brows drawn low and tight over his eyes. "How?"

Alex gave her classic little shrug. "I had a fall. It was nothing."

"It was that bastard, Terminator, wasn't it?" he demanded. Her stubborn silence was enough of an answer. "Dammit, Alex, get rid of him! He's dangerous. I'll send you horses from the QF string if you need the rides that badly. I'll fix it with Rylan. I'll pay the bloody training fees myself."

"You won't," Alex snapped, her chin going up. The mounts she got, she got on her own.

"You deserve better, Alex!"

No, I don't. The thought came instantly, but she didn't put it into words. She turned away from him instead and pulled on her underwear.

Christian heaved a sigh and raked a hand back through his hair, tilting his head down. He was trying to run her life for her, and she was determined to be independent. He could understand her need to make it on her own, but in his heart, where new love was taking fragile root, he was terrified. He wanted to take care of Alex. He wanted to keep her safe. But she wouldn't let him.

Adding to his frustration was the fact that he had never wanted to interfere in anyone's life before. His old bachelor philosophies warred with these new desires, until his head pounded from the struggle.

"Don't let's fight," he said quietly, rubbing his temples. "It's been such a perfect afternoon."

Alex's temper evaporated like so much steam. Fighting was the last thing she wanted to do. She went directly into Christian's arms when he opened them to her.

They kissed, each desperate to reassure the other that all was forgiven. And as they sank back down to the blanket, the fight was forgotten and paradise was revisited.

Eight

The day began with a heat wave and a dozen red roses. The heat now permeated everything, making a mockery of the efforts of the groaning old fan Alex had stuck in her bedroom window. The roses now stood in their cut-glass vase, elegant and out of place on the old walnut dresser in the tiny beige-walled bedroom.

Next had come the dress. It was now being arranged over her lithe body by her fairy godmothers, Maggie Quaid and Katie Leone, while Alex fidgeted from black-stockinged foot to black-stockinged foot.

Katie and Nick had volunteered to take Isabella for the night, since Pearl had been called away to spend a few days with one of her nieces, who had just had some minor surgery. Katie and Maggie had shown up together just as Alex had been taking the dress out of its protective bag. They had both insisted on seeing her in it before they left.

"It's gorgeous, Alex," Katie murmured, zipping up the low back. "You say Christian just had it delivered?"

Alex nibbled at her lower lip nervously, frowning at her reflection. She stood on the lumpy green-brocade footstool that had been pilfered from the living room so she could see most of herself in the mirror above the dresser. Her bangs spilled over her forehead in a riot of humidity-enhanced curls. Heavy gold hoops hung from her earlobes. She was wearing makeup for the first time in ages and wondered absently if it would all just melt off before she got where she was going.

"I told him I didn't have anything to wear to this party at Green Hills," she said, shrugging expressively. "He said he wasn't going to let me get away with that tired old line. This morning *this* shows up by special delivery," she said, twitching the royal blue flounced skirt.

"How do you like that?" Maggie said dryly, planting her hands on her hips. "He sends you this fabulous dress just for a date. Do y'all know what Rylan gave me for my birthday this year? A garden weasel. You know, one of those hoe things with the spiky teeth on it." She shook her head in woeful resignation. "He's the soul of romance, isn't he?"

She sounded disgusted, but as usual when she talked about her husband, her face lit up with a loving glow.

They all turned their attention back to Alex's reflection in the mirror, including Isabella, who was playing on the bed. Her dark eyes grew round with wonder as she stared at her mother.

"Isn't Mama pretty?" Katie said, sitting on the brown quilted spread and letting Isabella scramble onto her lap. The baby, clad only in a diaper because of the heat, immediately grabbed the end of Katie's long braid and tickled her nose with it.

"Don't you think it's a little too . . ." Alex's hands fluttered helplessly as words failed her. She felt naked. She hadn't worn anything so . . . provocative . . . in a long time. It felt foreign and forbidden.

"Good heavens, sugar." Maggie clucked. "It doesn't even show any cleavage." She sounded vaguely disappointed in Christian's lack of foresight.

"That's because I haven't got any," Alex declared. She skimmed her hands across the black sequins that covered her stomach, her brows pulling together in concern. "Don't you think it's a little . . . snug?"

"It's perfect," Maggie announced with a note of

finality as she adjusted the large taffeta bow at Alex's hip. "You're a pretty young lady, going out with a man most women would give their eyeteeth for, Alex. Why not show off a little bit?"

Because she'd spent the past eighteen months trying to hide herself and her femininity, Alex thought. What had begun as a concerted effort had become second nature to her. She would have felt much more at ease in an oversize shirt and a baggy pair of jeans.

She stared at herself and tried to be objective. It *was* lovely. Whisper-thin straps led down over her shoulders to a simple, fitted bodice of shimmering black sequins that hugged her slender body, nipping in at her tiny waist and stretching slightly over her slim hips. The skirt was of royal blue taffeta edged in fine black lace. It was attached in a wrap-around style set at a sassy angle higher on her left hip, where the bow was perched, and lower on her right. There really wasn't anything revealing about it. It was tasteful and chic and obviously expensive.

"Don't you think it might be too fancy?" she asked, determined to find a reason not to wear it. "This is an outdoor party."

"Honey, when Hayden Hill puts on a party, there is no such thing as too fancy," Maggie said. "I heard they set up a tent big enough to hold a three-ring circus, which is probably what it will be. A black-tie, ball-gown circus. If I thought I had a snowball's chance of squeezing myself into that dress, I'd go in your place." She stood back and heaved a sigh up into her damp red bangs. "We were invited, but I couldn't get Rylan there with a twenty-mule hitch." She rolled her dark eyes expressively. "He still thinks Carter Hill has eyes for me. Can y'all believe that?" Shaking her head, she patted her rounded tummy through the madras-plaid cotton maternity jumper she wore.

Alex broke out of her apprehensive mood with a sparkling laugh as she hopped down from the foot-stool in a rustle of taffeta. It had been so long since she'd had real friends, she had forgotten what it was like to get together with them and gossip and tease. The wary shyness she had cultivated since the attack hadn't stopped the gregarious Maggie from taking her into her fold of friends. Nor had it deterred sensible, sweet Katie in any way. If either of them suspected she had a dark secret in her past, they didn't mention it, or they respected her right to keep it. They got together to chat as regularly as their various schedules allowed. They had even begun doing things together as couples.

Couples, Alex thought with a little shiver of excitement. She and Christian were a couple. It seemed so strange after she had convinced herself she would be alone indefinitely. He came over nearly every evening to help her or to cajole her into going into Briarwood with him for a cup of cappuccino at Nick's, or a movie or a walk around the small town's historic district, where a number of old homes had been restored and beautiful gardens overflowed with vibrant color and sweet fragrances.

Many nights Isabella accompanied them, but they had managed to get a few evenings all to themselves, and those had been magic. Christian was a wonderful lover. Under his devoted tutelage Alex found herself rediscovering her sexuality and reveling in it. She found herself falling more in love with him every day.

But with the love came a vague, distant sense of apprehension. She was afraid of becoming too dependent on him, too devoted to him. Experience had taught her to rely on no one and nothing, save herself. She couldn't afford to let Christian run her life or her business, because there was no guarantee that he would always be there. To Michael DeGrazia she had pledged her love and trust unto death, but he was now more than two thousand miles away, as far removed from her life as the moon.

"Look at the time," Maggie said, checking her watch. "I have to get out of here before Christian comes. The sight of that man in a tuxedo is enough to make me swoon." She leaned over and gave Alex an affectionate hug, made awkward by her bulk. "Y'all have fun now, honey, and that's an order—as my daddy the admiral always says."

"Thanks, Maggie. Katie, you're sure Isabella won't be an imposition?"

"Don't be silly," Katie said, rising with the baby in her arms. "We'll have a great time with her. Besides, it'll be good practice. Nick and I are on a waiting list to adopt."

That was apparently a bombshell, if the startled look on Maggie's face was anything to go by, but there was no time to discuss it. The screen door banged, and Christian's voice called out.

"Alex?"

With Isabella perched on her slim hip, Katie led the way out of the bedroom, as calm as if she'd just said she and Nick were getting a puppy. Maggie followed, bubbling over with curiosity. Alex trailed behind with a stomach full of butterflies.

Christian looked the part of the consummate gentleman in his pleated white dress shirt and black bow tie. No one would have guessed by looking at him that it was ninety-plus degrees. He looked cool and sophisticated, too well-bred to sweat. His tuxedo was the absolute latest in chic European styles with a double-breasted jacket that enhanced his lean handsomeness. He definitely belonged somewhere more glamorous than her shabby little kitchen with its cracked gray linoleum and outdated appliances, Alex thought.

Her breath fluttered out of her as their gazes locked. Christian smiled, a slow, devastatingly sexy smile. It generated a fire inside Alex that made the hot day seem like a day in Antarctica.

"Exquisite," he murmured, his sapphire eyes glowing with male appreciation as they scanned Alex from head to toe.

"Don't mind us homely stepsisters," Katie said, grabbing up Alex's diaper bag from the Formica tabletop. "We were just leaving. Come on along now, Mary Margaret."

Maggie was swaying on her feet, staring raptly at Christian and fanning herself with a pot holder she'd picked up from the counter.

"Maggie?" Katie called, tugging at the short sleeve of her friend's pink T-shirt. "Oh, Maggie!"

"You'll have to drive, sugar," she mumbled, fishing in her patch pocket for her keys. "I feel positively overcome."

Isabella took the keys and rattled them merrily.

"Say good-bye, Maggie," Katie said, heading for the door.

"Good-bye, Maggie."

"Bye-bye!" Isabella called, shaking the keys.

Tearing herself away from Christian's magnetism, Alex rushed to the door to thank her friends again and to kiss her daughter good-bye. Feeling the return of the jitters, she watched through the screen door as they drove away in Maggie's blue station wagon.

"I hope Isabella is good for Katie and Nick. She hasn't been sleeping well."

"She'll be fine," Christian murmured, slipping his arms around her from behind and bending down to kiss her neck. "And so will you, darling."

Sometimes the man was too darn perceptive for his own good, Alex thought. He knew she was nervous about attending the Hills' party. Everybody who was anybody in show jumping would be there. She was gradually getting over the feeling that everybody in the world knew about her past, but the equestrian community was a relatively small one. There was a very good chance that she would eventually run into someone who knew. She dreaded the thought.

"I am so very anxious to show you off," Christian murmured, taking his arms from around her waist. A few seconds later he was fastening a necklace around her throat.

"Christian!" Alex said in protest as she fingered

the beautiful piece. A vee of dark sapphires rested against her skin just above the neckline of her dress. The gold herringbone chain gleamed against her dark skin. "You've given me way too much already!"

Turning her, he took her in his arms again and bent toward her lips. "I haven't given you even half of what's in my heart," he murmured as he settled his mouth over hers and kissed her deeply, with a hunger that never left him.

A low, rapturous sound rumbled deep in his throat as Alex rose up on tiptoe and twined her arms around his neck, tilting her head to give him better access. He trailed the kiss down the slender column of her throat to the spot where it joined her shoulder and nibbled at her smooth skin around the chain of necklace. Passion leapt to life instantly, a flame that would never be extinguished between them, but with it came something sweeter and softer—the glow of love.

There was still a part of him that shuddered at the thought of committing himself to one woman. But the tremors were gradually becoming weaker as his old rakish tendencies gave way to other feelings. With a certain sense of resignation Christian realized that he was becoming positively domestic.

As he held Alex to him, he murmured a little apology to dearly departed Uncle Dicky. The last of the Atherton black sheep was fading into respectability.

The lawn at Green Hills looked like an emerald carpet liberally dotted with the colors of party-goers—men in their formal black and white, women standing out like jewels among them in their richly colored evening wear. There was indeed an enormous green-and-white-striped tent, the sides of which had been rolled up to let through whatever cooling breeze the evening might bring. Under the big top was a lavish buffet with barbecued beef and pork, platters of fresh fruit, and seafood presented on beds of shaved ice. The bar had been set up directly across from the buffet and was doing a lively business, the heat and the conversation drumming up thirsts all around. One end of the shelter held a number of long tables draped in white and adorned with trailing green ivy plants for centerpieces. The remainder of the space beneath the tent was taken up by a portable dance floor. A five-piece combo nestled into one corner, playing contemporary hits, classics, and standards.

The level of energy and opulence about the place was impressive and infectious. The following day the show horses would take center stage. At present it was their owners and trainers who provided the spectacle.

Alex recognized some of the faces from the smaller shows she had been attending. Others she knew on sight from their photographs in the magazines— Katie Prudent and Debbie Shaffner, Greg Best and George Morris and Rodney Jenkins. Hayden Hill's party was a virtual *Who's Who* of show jumping. It was a thrill to rub shoulders with them, and an even bigger thrill to remember that Christian resided at the top of their ranks.

The pair of them turned a lot of heads. It became apparent very quickly to Alex that more than one of the ladies in attendance coveted her date. Feminine gazes followed them with interest and envy, clinging to Christian's elegant person. He either didn't notice or had grown so accustomed to female scrutiny that it no longer fazed him. It certainly fazed Alex. She didn't like the idea of other women homing in on her date. And she felt a horrendous surge of jealousy when she realized that more than one of those ladies probably knew Christian on intimate terms, given his reputation.

I'm in love with him, she thought with renewed wonder as she watched him laugh at something Carter Hill had said. She'd known it for days, of course. If she was honest with herself, she would have to say she'd been in love with him since that day in the meadow, or even before that. She'd been attracted to him from the first. The day he'd held her after she told him about her past had tipped her heart over the edge. How could she not love him when he had given her the kind of unqualified support not even her husband had been able to manage? He hadn't rejected her or blamed her or found her fundamentally flawed in some irreparable way.

He had told her he loved her, but she hadn't quite let herself believe it. Words like love came easily to men like Christian. And a part of Alex just couldn't quite believe her life could include the handsome, wealthy son of an earl. It was just too good. What had she done to deserve him? She kept thinking there had to be a catch, that eventually the other shoe would drop. But what if he really meant it? What if what they had between them was truly something special?

A shiver of hope ran through her, pebbling her skin in spite of the heat of the Virginia evening.

"All set for tomorrow, honey?" Tully Haskell's voice boomed down on her from above.

Alex jolted out of her trance and turned to look up at him. Tully's version of black tie was a black, western-cut suit and a bolo tie snugged up to his flabby throat. The overall effect might have been trendy and stylish on a younger, trimmer man. Tully tainted it toward the vulgar. He clutched a champagne glass and one of his omnipresent cigars in one hand, leaving the other free to pat Alex's bare shoulder.

She moved away from his touch on the pretense of changing position and gave him the most businesslike smile she could scrape together. "I hope so, Mr. Haskell. Duchess will handle everything well. I'm afraid we may be asking Terminator to do too much too soon."

"Nonsense," Tully barked, his mouth tightening, eyes flashing for the briefest instant.

Alex didn't miss the look, though she erased it quickly. Tully didn't like her questioning his authority. He had been determined his horses would perform in the Green Hills show. They were his ticket into the realm of the sport's elite. He didn't care how his decision affected the horses. With Tully the end always justified the means. So went the relationship between owners and trainers. Some were reasonable and understanding. The majority wanted miracles worked at bargain rates.

"Don't you look pretty tonight, Alex," he said, eyeing her appreciatively. "By golly, I believe this is the first time I've seen you dressed up like a woman. Looks damn good on you."

The backhanded compliment couldn't inspire a thank you from Alex. Every doubt she'd had about wearing the dress rushed back to her with a vengeance. Instead of feeling lovely and special, she felt cheap. She was suddenly overcome by the feeling that the makeup she had applied so sparingly was as overdone as a ten-dollar tramp's.

Christian turned toward her to say something, but the words died on his tongue as he took in the look on her face. All he had to do was glance up to find the root cause of her tension.

"I say," he drawled, lifting his nose in disdain. "Aren't they checking the invitations at the gate?"

"Read it and weep, you arrogant limey bastard," Tully growled, plucking his engraved invitation out of the inner pocket of his jacket and waving it tauntingly in Christian's face.

"Really," Christian said, putting on every snobbish air that had been bred into countless generations of Athertons, "the alarming decline of social standards is truly appalling."

Haskell sneered at him, handing his champagne glass to a passing waiter without even glancing at the man. "Yeah? Well, I don't give a rat's rump what you think. Eat that with your tea and crumpets, your lordship, while Alex gives me the pleasure of this next dance."

Alarm slammed Alex's heart against her breastbone like a paddle ball. Dance with Tully Haskell? Let Tully Haskell put his meaty paws all over her?

Her throat constricted as she fought the urge to gag.
The last thing she wanted to do was let down the
trainer/owner barrier she had struggled to main-
tain, even if it was only long enough for one brief
turn around the dance floor. But how could she
refuse the man without offending him?

He reached for her wrist, but Christian stopped
him, his fingers closing forcefully on Haskell's forearm. All traces of the dandy fell away from Christian
like a crumbling shield. He radiated power and
authority. The intense dislike he felt for the older
man was more than evident in the curl of his lip
and the steel in his eyes.

"Not if you value your precious, tenuous standing
in this group," he said with deadly quiet.

There was no need for him to raise his voice, Alex
thought with awe. The force of his personality was
enough to turn the heads of a number of people
nearby. Haskell might have been physically larger,
but he was no match for Christian in this kind of
a fight, and the quick darting of the man's dark
little eyes betrayed the fact that he knew it.

Contempt added another facet to Christian's
expression as he spoke again. "My connections
make yours look like so many knots in a ratty boot-
lace, Haskell. I wouldn't think twice about getting
you chucked out of here for trying to steal my date."

"Why don't you let the lady decide?" Tully said,
his gaze sliding to Alex with a mean gleam in them.

It was a classic damned-if-you-do, damned-if-you-
don't situation. Alex looked from one man to the
other and took the only option that made any sense
at all.

"If you gentlemen will excuse me, I have to go powder my nose."

She crossed the lawn with the steady flow of
guests going to and from the Hills' red-brick Geor-
gian mansion. Taking her time, she browsed
through the entry hall, eventually making her way
to the line for the rest room, where she exchanged
idle chat with several ladies about the ruinous

effects of heat and humidity on hairdos. When she hiked back toward the tent some time later, her heels punching down into the finely manicured lawn, she hoped cooler male heads had prevailed.

Tully had taken root where she'd left him, no doubt awaiting her return. But before he could spot her, Christian intercepted her and steered her in a different direction.

Alex frowned at him, her full lower lip pouting in disapproval. "I wish you wouldn't bait Haskell that way."

Christian made a face. "He's a pompous, over-blown bully—"

"Who pays his training bills on time."

"You know how I feel about that."

"Yes. And you know how I feel about it."

"Then there's no point in discussing it, is there?" He shrugged off his bad mood and treated her to one of his fabulous smiles, complete with twinkling blue eyes. "You can't blame me for wanting you all to myself, can you, darling? You are, by far, the most dazzling beauty here tonight."

"You're a liar," Alex said, sparkling at his compliment, "but I love the way you do it."

"Do you?" The heat in his gaze went up ten degrees as he pulled her closer, one hand settling possessively on the small of her back. "Well, we both have something to look forward to later on then, don't we?" he murmured, the slow curving of his mouth so frankly sensual, it made Alex's pulse rate pick up a beat. He stared at her as if there weren't two hundred other people milling around them talking and laughing, as if he wanted to take her right there and then and make wild, sweet love to her.

Alex's nerve endings hummed with sexual awareness. All it ever took from him was a look, a word, a touch, and she was on fire for him. It was an addiction, an obsession, and she was powerless to stop it, helpless even to fight against it.

"Dance with me," he commanded, taking her hands in his.

Alex glanced toward the band. "But there's no one else dancing."

"Good."

He led her onto the dance floor, not allowing her to bow to her fears of drawing attention to herself. Still holding her hand, he leaned toward the female singer of the group, a woman with Jessica Lange's looks and Bette Midler's voice, and whispered a few words in her ear. When he drew back, the woman was smiling warmly.

"Everyone is staring at us," Alex muttered as Christian drew her reluctant body into his arms. She held herself formally stiff, refusing to snuggle against him the way he wanted her to.

"So they are," he said with an arrogant shrug. "Let them look their fill. What do I care? I only have eyes for you."

Looking up at him Alex nibbled at her lip, destroying her lipstick and not caring. She knew what he was saying, and she loved him for it. He didn't care who saw them or who knew about her past or what they thought about it. Her importance in his life far overshadowed theirs.

The band started the number with the slow, bluesy strains of a piano. And Alex's eyes filled with tears as the singer's voice started in, strong and smoky, singing from her soul. *When a Man Loves a Woman.*

Christian began moving, sensually, drawing Alex to him with his body and with the intensity of his gaze. His hands splayed over her hips, guiding her, inviting her.

As the drum and bass joined in, Alex slid her arms up around his neck and began moving with him, without reservation, without a thought to what anyone else might be thinking. Everyone else had ceased to exist, had faded away into the heat of the night. There were only Christian and herself and the sexy, heartfelt music that surrounded them with its sensual, steady beat. There were only the two of them and the music and the feelings that flowed between them and twined around them. And when the song faded away, she leaned up into his kiss, giving him her thanks without words, giving him her love.

What better time to tell him, she thought as her feet settled onto the floor. Her heart thumped with anticipation as she looked up at him. Her hands twisted themselves into a knot. "Christian, I—"

"Well, by golly, you did it, pal," a slightly inebriated Robert Braddock said as he slapped Christian on the shoulder. "Honest to Pete, I didn't think even you could pull it off, but you did."

"Do what?" Alex asked, a strange kind of foreboding flooding her. She stood a step or two back from Christian, unable to go to him because of Braddock.

"Robert," Christian said in a warning tone. He held himself absolutely still, as if that would somehow make Braddock lose interest and wander away. "Now is not the time."

"The time for what?" Alex's dark brows drew together in confusion and apprehension.

Braddock waved off his friend's suggestion as he took a gulp of champagne. "I'm a gentleman," he said, his voice slurring a bit. "A gentleman always makes good on his bets."

With his free hand he dug a wad of bills out of his pants pocket and stuffed them messily into Christian's breast pocket.

"One iceberg properly melted. You have my congratulations."

Suddenly the truth dawned, descending on Alex with a wave of numbing cold. Unfortunately the pain cut through it quickly, and she was besieged by equal blasts of hurt and humiliation. She had been the object of a wager. A challenge. A stray female to be speculated over and made sport of.

The other shoe had dropped with a resounding thud.

She stared at Christian, not wanting to believe the

guilt written all over his face. She loved him. He had battered down every defense she had. He had bullied and begged and bribed her into falling in love with him. And it had all been a game to him.

"Alex—" he began, reaching out toward her. The look in her eyes was ominous.

"You bastard!" She spat the word and slapped him across the face as hard as she could.

"Alex, wait!" he called, all too aware of the crowd that was staring and straining hungrily for any tidbit of gossip. Damn them all to perdition. What he had to say was no secret. "Alex, I love you!"

His words wrenched away the last shred of her control, and the tears she had tried so hard to hold at bay spilled over their barriers and streamed down her cheeks as she pushed her way through the crowd. Love. There wasn't any for her here. There wasn't any for her anywhere. She should have known better.

"Damn you, Braddock!" Christian wheeled on his fellow trainer.

Robert's brows rose over slightly unfocused eyes. "What'd I do?"

"Ruined my entire bloody life, that's all!" Christian bellowed. He pulled the prize money out of his pocket and threw it to the floor like so much scrap paper, then stamped on it with his elegant black Italian shoes.

"You mean you really do love her?" Braddock asked in classic bachelor amazement.

"I really do love her, you imbecile!"

"Well, shoot, Chris," he whined. "That's no fun."

Christian's hands lifted, intent on throttling the life out of his friend. He groaned with the effort to hold himself back, torn between sweet revenge and cursed respectability. Then his gaze caught the nearly full champagne glass Braddock held, and his hands changed their course.

With one he snatched the glass from Robert's hand. With the other he hooked the front of the man's trousers. The chilled champagne went down inside Braddock's pants in a freezing golden stream, but Christian didn't waste an extra second to catch the look on Robert's face. He had to find Alex.

Nine

Alex abandoned her shoes as soon as she had pushed through the party crowd. Barefoot, she ran across the lawn, away from the tent, away from the house. Her first impulse was to run to the stables, but as she caught sight of the lights she remembered that they were full of show horses and dozens of grooms. She veered instead for the row of dark buildings that sat behind the Hill mansion, the plantation dependencies that had been preserved for their historical value. Reaching the second one, which had once been the kitchen, she stopped running and slumped against the end of the brick building. With the moon on the other side she was swallowed up by the shadow the building cast. Enveloped in darkness, hidden from prying eyes, she was free to cry out all the hurt.

Why did this have to happen? She'd tried so hard to avoid being made a spectacle of again. Hadn't she? She couldn't think of a single thing she'd done to attract attention to herself since she'd moved to Briarwood. She hadn't gone asking for men to call on her. She'd done just the opposite, avoiding them, trying to discourage them.

And they had seen her as a challenge.

It *was* her fault.

She turned and pressed herself against the wall, the rough brick biting into her cheek and palms. And she sobbed, torn by abject, soul-wrenching misery. She sobbed for the things she'd lost, for the heart that lay broken in her breast, for the love she had that never seemed to find a worthy home. And she cried harder because she didn't understand the reasons why. She had never meant for any of it to happen. She tried to be a good person, tried to mind her own business. But why did these things keep happening to her then, if it wasn't something she did or said or thought?

Wiping back one wave of tears she looked down at the dress she wore, barely able to see the outline in the dark of the shadows. A hundred women could have worn it and felt special. She felt tainted, ashamed that she had ever put it on. She pushed her palms down the front of it, cringing as if it disgusted her, as if she could push it away and have her old baggy clothes magically appear in its stead. But the dress remained, tangible evidence for the old recriminations that came flooding back to ring in her ears.

"You're too flamboyant, Alexa."

"You're too sassy, Alexa."

"You were asking for it."

"But I wasn't!" she whispered in tortured anguish, pressing her hands to her face as the tears came fresh and hot.

She sobbed until she had no tears left to shed, until her head was throbbing and her eyes ached. And then she just stood there, exhausted, nothing left of her inner wall of strength but rubble. She sagged against the brick, not caring that it cut into the bare skin of her back, listening to the cicadas sing in the hot, fragrant summer night.

In the distance she could hear the band playing, the sound rising above the murmur of the crowd. The low thrum of the bass, the vibrant wail of the singer's voice, an occasional crash of a cymbal. Closing her eyes, she relived the dance she'd shared with Christian. For five glorious minutes she had been deliriously happy and in love, soaring higher than she ever could on a horse. And an instant later it had all come crashing down. The heart that had been bursting with joy now lay in a cold, crumbled ruin. The love she had been so ready to give was back inside its little locked box, not to be taken out again for a long, long time.

There were no more tears. Only a pure, piercing ache from which she knew there would be no escape.

The sound that came to her from nearby didn't penetrate immediately, not until she heard the low, rough voice of a man swearing under his breath. He'd bumped into something in the dark and was cursing. Alex brought herself to attention, her whole body straining to hear. He was at the first building in the row, the icehouse. She couldn't see him clearly but was able to distinguish his shape as he moved along the back side of the building where the darkness was intensified by a row of tall crape myrtle shrubs.

Her traitorous heart gave a lurch at the thought that it might be Christian coming to find her. She dismissed both the thought and the sentiment as she inched along the wall intending to slip around the front side of the kitchen, where she would be completely out of view to the man who was approaching. Christian wouldn't come skulking up the back of the buildings if he was looking for her. He would come striding up the path like a prince, demanding in that autocratic tone of voice that she come out of hiding. At any rate, he wouldn't come looking for her. His game was up. Anyone else who had a reason for stalking around in the shadows Alex had no desire to meet.

She glanced at the bright moonlight that fell on the path. She would be in plain sight for an instant as she moved around to the other side of the building. Old instincts of flight and self-preservation rose up inside her as the crape myrtle trees rustled just fifteen feet away. She realized with a stroke of chilling fear just how vulnerable she was, far removed from the party and the safety of the crowd. Beyond these unused buildings lay nothing but dense forest.

Christian, if he even cared, had probably decided she'd caught a lift home. No one would miss her until morning.

Swallowing down the knot of fear in her throat, Alex took one last glance in the direction of the man and slipped around the edge of the building. As she turned to run she slammed head-on into a wall of masculinity. Gasping, too terrified to scream, she bolted backward only to be caught in his arms and held.

"Alex!" Christian exclaimed, his relief plain in his voice. "Thank God! I've been searching everywhere for you!"

She said nothing but darted a nervous glance in the direction of the icehouse. Whoever had been there was gone. The trees were still. It had probably been one of the gentlemen too impatient to wait in line for the rest room.

"Darling, we've got to talk."

"What's there to say?" Alex asked tiredly. "It seemed pretty self-explanatory to me. I won you a nice wad of money. You should be happy."

"Oh, hang Robert and his stupid bet," Christian said fiercely, unwittingly tightening his grip on her upper arms. "It's got nothing to do with us."

"Oh, really?" Alex arched a brow. Her tone was one of icy sarcasm. "I think it's got quite a lot to do with me. The Italian Iceberg—isn't that what your pals call me?" she asked bitterly. "You'll be quite the hero with them now, won't you? But of course, you're already a legend among their ranks. How many notches on your bedpost are there now that you can count me?"

"Dammit, Alex, stop it!" Christian said, shaking her. "It's not like that!"

She stared up at him as she wrenched herself free of his hold. "Isn't it?"

"I forgot about the bloody bet as soon as I'd met you."

"Sure, you did," she said with a sneer. "That's why you were so insistent about me going out with you. That's why you hounded me until I agreed to come to this stupid party with you." She enumerated his sins, ticking them off one by one on her fingers. A new supply of tears rose as she glanced down at herself. The shimmer of sequins and taffeta was like moonlight reflected on a lake. "Your pride must have really been on the line for you to go to all the trouble of buying this dress. You had to have lost money on the deal."

Christian ground his teeth at her stubborn refusal to listen. It pricked his pride to think how quickly she'd believed the worst of him, how quickly she had discounted everything that had passed between them. "Do you honestly think if I'd remembered the bet, I would have subjected you to that scene on the dance floor?"

"No," she murmured and smiled ruefully at his sigh of relief. "You're much too British for that. You might be a bastard, but your manners are impeccable."

"Alex—"

"Frightfully bad form on Robert's part, though, wasn't it?" she said, mimicking his upper-crust accent.

Christian's broad shrug was a gesture of supplication. "Alex, what do I have to say to make you believe me when I tell you I love you?"

"There isn't anything you can say. I've seen just how much you love me—enough to bet me to win."

She reached behind her to the nape of her neck, unfastened the heavy gold chain of her necklace, and held it out on her upturned palm for Christian to take. The fight draining out of her, she murmured, "I'll send the dress back tomorrow."

Christian looked at the coil of gold and dark stones in her hand but didn't reach out for it. His heart ached abominably. There was a horrid pressure behind his eyes. Gads, this love business stank to high heaven! His life had been so much less complicated before. There was a great deal to be said for being a carefree bachelor. Affairs were light and fun with clean breaks at the end of them. There would be no clean break with Alex. It would be ragged and bloody, and when Alex left, she would be dragging his heart with her by the ties of love that had bound him to her. He'd never felt so desperate in his life.

He stared into her eyes feeling bleak and lost and guilty. Guilty! Blast it, he hadn't known what guilt was until he'd met Alex! She had him feeling it on a regular basis. Why should he want to go on enduring that?

Because he loved her.

He loved her, and she was going to walk away.

She had managed to arrange her face into the cool, emotionless mask he remembered from when they'd first met. Slowly she turned her hand over, and the necklace spilled to the ground in a river of glimmering gold. He watched it fall and felt it in his heart when it hit the grass.

"Alex, don't do this." He whispered because he didn't trust his voice. He kept his head down and his eyes trained on the ground, because he didn't know what would happen to him if he watched her turn and go.

"Just tell me one thing," Alex said, needing to know more than she needed to flee. "Is there something about me . . . something I did . . .?"

The only thing that could have cut through Christian's own pain was Alex's. His concern for her had overridden his own selfish needs almost from the first. So his head came up at the strain in her voice, the uncertainty, the hurt. Each of those emotions was reflected in the depths of her wide, dark eyes. Her lush mouth trembled with vulnerability.

Good Lord, she was blaming herself for this fiasco! If he ever got his hands on Robert Braddock again, he wouldn't try to keep from throttling the bastard, he'd do the job proper, then dance on his grave.

"Alex, the bet was nothing more than an idiotic challenge between two overgrown adolescents who should have had sense enough to know better. I didn't see the harm in it. I thought we'd get to know each other, go out, have a few laughs. I didn't count on falling in love with you. I've never been in love," he admitted plaintively. "I'd say it's bloody awful right about now, but I do love you, I can't stand the idea of you not believing me!"

She wanted to believe him. In spite of all the pain and all the doubts, Alex knew she wanted to believe in him. It wasn't a comforting thought. He'd made a fool of her. He'd made her doubt herself. He'd crushed her heart.

Memories came back to make a bid on Christian's behalf. He had listened to the story of her ordeal with compassion and sympathy. He'd held her while she'd cried. He had reawakened her to the joys that could be shared by a man and woman. He'd made her feel like someone special again, like a woman, like someone to be cherished and delighted in instead of someone to be ashamed of and embarrassed by. He'd held her in front of everyone in their world and made it more than clear that his feelings ran deep, that he didn't care who knew it or what they thought.

When a Man Loves a Woman.

Heaven help her, how badly she wanted that to be true.

She looked up at him with her heart in her eyes, the moonlight catching her full in the face, stark and white, hiding no secrets, hiding no tears. Christian stepped closer, holding her gaze with his. He lifted his hands to cup her face, his thumbs gently brushing along her cheekbones. Moving closer still, he slid his palms slowly down the column of her throat, over her shoulders, and down her bare back. His fingers traced the low vee in the back of her gown and pressed gently, drawing her near.

"I love you, Alex." He murmured the words against her lips, feathered them along her cheek, brushed them across her forehead. He pulled her full against him in an embrace that was both fierce and tender and whispered into the lush, scented mass of curls atop her head. "Believe me. Please, believe me."

Alex pressed her cheek to his chest. Through the warm, damp fabric of his dress shirt she could feel the solid strength of him. She could hear his heart beating a little quickly as he waited for her answer. Wrapping her arms around his lean waist she hugged herself to him. It might have been smarter to walk away. It might have been safer to leave him. But the thought of living without him, of going back to the life she'd had before him, was so cold and lonely. If there was a chance he could love her, she needed to take it.

"Alex?"

He whispered her name so softly, she might have imagined it. "Yes," she answered, just as softly. "I believe you."

The music drifted from speakers that were built into the bookshelves in the bedroom wall. Soft, smoky, sexy, as hot as the night itself, it twined around the couple dancing in the dark, weaving them into the magic, seeping into their souls.

When a Man Loves a Woman . . .

Christian had left his coat tossed carelessly in the back seat of the Mercedes along with Alex's pantyhose. His tie was gone, as were the studs from his shirt front. The garment hung open, exposing the smooth, hard planes of his chest. Alex arched herself against him. Her arms were wrapped around his neck, his banded around the small of her back, lifting her into him. Together they swayed to the sensual beat. Thigh brushing thigh, breast to chest, every move was a caress, each caress leading to another, with no sound except the music and the soft rustle of fabric.

The moon spilled its silver light through the sheer curtain at the window. The breeze stirred the curtain to a dance of its own. The sultry heat that hung thick in the air was as much a product of the mood as it was of the sun. It rose from their entwined bodies, from the intensity of their gaze, as Christian looked down into Alex's face, and Alex tilted her head back and stared up into Christian's hot blue eyes. It steamed around them as Christian settled his mouth against hers in a deep kiss.

Tongues dancing, twining, sliding over each other, they tasted and savored the flavor of love, a flavor made sweeter by having nearly lost it. Alex let her hands set off on an exploration of Christian's chest, taking joy in the simple pleasure of touching him. As the angle of the kiss altered, she slid her fingers over the slick hot skin of his belly, dipping inside the opened waistband of his black trousers, teasing.

Trailing his mouth down Alex's jaw to the arched column of her throat, Christian slid the straps of her dress down until they dangled against her arms. With just the tips of his fingers he stroked the satin skin of her shoulders, drawing a sigh from her. The sigh deepened to a moan as his hands slid down over the curve of her back and softened to another sigh as the zipper of her dress whispered its descent. His fingers splayed across her hips as the taffeta skirt rustled to the floor, leaving Alex naked in his arms.

She let her head fall back as he lifted her to him, reveling in the feel of her breasts caressing his chest and the dark delta of curls that protected her femininity rubbing against his belly. He turned with her in his arms and lowered her gently to the cool cotton sheets of the big mahogany four-poster bed. She lay back against the mountain of pillows and watched as he lowered the zipper of his trousers and stepped out of them, then lowered his snug briefs and dropped them to the thick ruby carpet that stretched across the polished pine floor.

He came to her the perfect example of the male animal—sleek, hard muscled, beautifully aroused. His gaze was on her face, reading every nuance of her desire, telegraphing the intense quality of his. His fine, silky hair spilled across his forehead. A bead of sweat trickled down the center of his chest.

The bed dipped beneath his weight as he settled one knee on the mattress and slid toward Alex.

Before he even touched her she felt him, felt that awesome power that radiated from him, and a thrill of excitement went through her.

He leaned over her, bracing himself up on his left arm as his right hand glided up her leg. Bending down to kiss her, he caught her sighs with his mouth as he stroked the heated core of her femininity with his thumb. Alex lifted her hips off the mattress, arching into his caress, begging for deeper contact. And she whimpered in frustration when he took his touch away. But then his mouth was on her breast, and her attention focused on the exquisite sensations there—the tingling that came with each tug of his hot, wet mouth on her nipple, the sparks that shot through her as his teeth grazed her flesh. He made her forget everything when he made love to her. She forgot the past, forgot her inhibitions, forgot everything but him and the beautiful, sensuous harmony they created together.

The music rambled on, bluesy and soulful, mingling with the sighs and moans of the dancers and the whisper of skin against sheets. The breeze blew in hot and sultry with the promise of a storm. Thunder rumbled somewhere over the mountains, but they didn't hear it. They were too caught up in the expression of feelings that went soul-deep, too caught up in the music.

When a Man Loves a Woman . . .

Christian trailed his mouth down Alex's belly, tasting her skin. His tongue dipped into her navel, skimmed lower, stroked languidly at the sweet, hot flower of her femininity. Alex's chest heaved as she gasped for a breath of the humid air. She tangled a hand in Christian's hair and moaned as she arched up, sliding one bare foot up and down his sweat-slicked back. The pleasure built, taking her higher and higher, but never over the edge.

Pulling away, he rolled her onto her belly and

kissed his way up the backs of her thighs, over the swell of her buttocks to the sensitive indentation at the small of her back, where he planted a slow kiss. He slid over her in a full body caress, settling himself intimately between her legs as he bent to nibble at the side of her throat.

"I need you, Alex," he murmured darkly, nuzzling her ear. "I need to be inside you, to feel you around me. I've never needed anything—anyone—the way I need you."

With the admission came a piercing shaft of fear deep inside him. Alex had become a part of him. No other woman had ever gotten so close. No other woman had ever held such power to hurt him. No other woman had ever stirred within him such a savage need to possess and protect. No other woman but this woman.

When a Man Loves a Woman . . .

She twisted beneath him, arching up, seeking contact. "I need you too," she whispered, turning her head to brush her lips across his. "Take me, Christian. Take me to paradise again."

They rolled across the bed then, Christian ending up with Alex draped over him, the heat of her pressing against his belly, her hands on either side of his head. Her head was thrown back, her breasts thrust magnificently forward. Christian arched up to take one mauve point into his mouth, and she wrapped her arms around him, holding him there until she finally pulled away, panting.

"I love you, Alex," he said with a growl, easing her down on his shaft.

Alex held her breath as he filled her with his strength, with his essence. Her body stretched and tightened around him, clutching him deep within her where she wanted him most, where she needed him so urgently. She lifted herself and slid down on him, slowly, prolonging the sensation. He kissed her, his mouth hot, avid, slanting hungrily across hers, his tongue plunging into her.

It was indescribable—the wondrous, mysterious, frightening sensation of being locked intimately with the man she loved. They were so close, so in tune. The physical expression of their feelings was so beautiful, it battered down the barriers inside her, reached straight to her heart. And she shivered a little at the thought of what awesome power this man held over her. She did her best to ignore the little voice that tried to tell her she shouldn't have let him so close, that she shouldn't love him so much, that she didn't deserve this kind of happiness. She shut out those dark thoughts that were trying to drift into her mind like smoke. Moving strongly on Christian, she took him deep and hard and gasped as the exquisite explosion of feeling obliterated all else.

Christian's control broke as lightning flashed over the distant hills and Alex's body stroked over his, taut as a bowstring, slick with sweat, trembling with building passion. She was the woman he loved—the only woman he'd ever truly loved with everything that was in his heart, with all that made up the man he was. He had nearly lost her, and the fear of that realization shot through him again as he held her to him.

With a desperate need to make her his, to brand her again with his possession, he rolled her beneath him and drove himself into her, urgent and frightened in a way he had never known before. Love reached past the pleasant surface emotions he'd shared with other women. It cut deeper than the heart, touched his soul, changed him forever in a way he could never begin to understand.

He looked down into Alex's face, no more than a breath away, into the glowing amber of her eyes, and saw his own feelings reflected back. They both groaned together as rapture built to a fever pitch and took them over the crest. Then they held each other, spent and sweating, tangled in the sheets, their sighs trailing off to melt into the music, their feelings hanging thick in the sultry air around them.

When a man loves a woman.

And in the still of the night the storm rumbled closer.

Ten

"Bloody beggar tried to bite me!" Charlie exclaimed indignantly as she dashed out of Terminator's stall and slammed shut the lower half of the door, her hasty actions belying the truculent look on her face. "Tried to take me arm right off, he did, the bleedin' sod!"

She gave the horse her meanest look, narrowing her eyes until they were mere slits between scowling brows and pudgy rouged cheeks. She shook a finger at the wild-eyed gelding. "Next stop's the canning factory, mind you."

"And it can't happen soon enough, as far as I'm concerned," Christian muttered.

He stood in the aisle, dressed for his first competition of the day in buff breeches and a pristine white shirt, which would not remain pristine for long. The storm that had rumbled through during the night had done nothing to alleviate the stifling heat but had managed to add another level of thickness to the humidity. It had also left the top layer of ground just wet enough to make mud—guaranteeing tricky footing in the ring and plenty of work for the grooms and the laundry services.

It was not yet midmorning, and already the temperature had climbed into the high eighties. Tempers had climbed in direct proportion. There were a great many more raised voices in the stables than usual, more horses with pinned ears, more grooms grumbling about menial tasks. Hanging on the grill-

work of many stalls were big square electric fans,
humming incessantly in an effort to keep the horses
cool. There was nothing to be done about the
human tempers. They rose and fell as sporadically
as the sultry breeze, adding their staccato accents
to the sounds of steel-shod hooves on concrete and
rock music blasting from a tape player.

"Are you all right?" Christian asked, eyeing the
girl.

Charlie flashed him an acrimonious look, the trio
of silver earrings on her right ear clanging together
like warning bells. She waited to speak until a pair
of junior hunters had been led past. As soon as their
handlers were out of earshot, she lit into her
employer. "A lot you care. Bloody well glad to be rid
of me, you are. And using me to do your dirty work
without me even knowing." She sneered at him,
clearly expressing her opinion of him as a life form
lower than pond scum. "You're a right flaming cad,
you are. No better than that horse," she said, jerking
a thumb over her shoulder at Terminator, who
pinned his ears and shook his head. "Worse, even.
At least he shows his colors."

Christian scowled. News traveled at the speed of
sound through the ranks of the grooms. No doubt
the nasty little scene he and Alex and Robert had
played out at the party had made its way to every
corner of the show grounds by now. It was probably
the hot topic over doughnuts at the concession
stand. The show secretaries were probably buzzing
about it in their little office. It was a wonder the
recapped version hadn't come over the PA system
with the morning announcements.

He heaved a sigh and planted his fists at his waist.
Guilt dug a talon into him at the thought that Charlie was more than half-right that he was using her.
Contrite or not, he wasn't going to admit that to
her, but he was going to set her straight as far as
his relationship with Alex went.

"I know what the rumors are, Charlotte," he said,
all traces of the flip, charming rogue gone. He looked

as serious as any of his stuffy brothers. "I also know what the facts are. I care very deeply for Alex. Feel free to spread that little bit of news around to all your gossiping friends."

Charlie rubbed a hand across her chin and gave him a long, measuring look. Finally she shrugged one shoulder and tugged up the strap of her orange tank top. "Maybe I will." She dragged the words out grudgingly.

Christian watched her scuff the toe of her sneaker against the concrete as she slid her hands into the pockets of baggy khaki shorts, and realized with a start that he wanted the girl's respect. Gads, he was turning into a bona fide Atherton! Respectability, responsibility, love. He sighed and shrugged, conceding defeat.

"You're looking grim," Alex said cheerfully, tapping him on the seat of his breeches with her crop as she sauntered in from the show office. She was dressed much the same as Christian was in buff breeches and a white blouse. Her blouse was sleeveless, a concession to the heat. Christian's sleeves were rolled neatly to his elbows, displaying strong tan arms and an expensive platinum watch. Her gaze lingered appreciatively on the way his breeches clung to the muscles of his thighs.

"It's this bloody heat," Christian grumbled, leaning down to kiss her lightly. "And the thought of you facing a grand prix course on that rabid animal."

Alex sighed and speared a hand back through her damp hair. "Let's not start on that, please."

Christian ground his teeth and glared at the chestnut. "He just tried to attack Simmonds."

"Are you okay?" Alex asked the groom, taking in the belligerent set of the girl's chin as well as the brief flash of uncertainty in her eyes. Charlie liked to play it tougher than she was. They had a lot in common that way.

"I'm fine. The guv'nor's stretching it a bit," she said evenly, her gaze steady on Christian's face.

"The bloody pig tried to bite me, is all. He does that every flippin' day."

At least he had to admire the girl's loyalty to Alex, Christian thought, rubbing at the tension in the back of his neck.

Alex looked into Terminator's stall, pensive as she stared at the horse. He was restless, weaving back and forth in front of his grain box in a habit that had schizophrenic overtones. His washy chestnut coat was already dark with sweat in patches along his neck and flank. The tension rolled off him in waves.

He wasn't ready for a show of this kind. He had earned his way into it, having accumulated a substantial amount of prize money during his checkered career. He had demonstrated to Alex that he could handle the fences, but his temperament had worsened with every increase in competition. A show like this one carried a certain excitement in the air. The grooms were busier, the general bustle in the stable was increased. The show grounds were alive with spectators, all of them excited about the caliber of horses and competition they were there to see. And the riders transmitted a nervous tension of their own. This wasn't some penny-ante schooling show with little fake gold cups for prizes. This was the highest echelon of competition. The horses here were worth tens of thousands and even hundreds of thousands of dollars. The riders were people who had competed internationally, people who had ridden in the Olympics. The prize money for the grand prix was fifty thousand dollars.

No, it wasn't that Terminator couldn't handle the fences. He couldn't handle the pressure. Alex knew it. She also knew that his owner would pack up Terminator and his stable mate and take them to another trainer if she scratched him from the competition.

Her gaze slid to the next stall where A Touch of Dutch stood on the far side, placidly submitting to the ministrations of the two Heathers, dozing as she enjoyed the breeze from the fan that was hooked to the box adjacent to hers.

"I can get you five that are her equal and better," Christian said softly, standing so close behind her, she could feel his body heat. "She's not the issue here, Alex."

No. The issue was her independence, Alex thought. This had to do with paying her dues and working her way up and not relying on anyone else for her livelihood or her success. It had to do with fighting demons and winning. Christian was asking her to lean on him, and she couldn't do it. She loved him, but she couldn't let herself allow him to save her, because she couldn't allow herself to believe he would be there the next time.

"I've got two in the pregreen class in an hour," she murmured, not looking up at him. "I'd better get cracking."

He raised his hands and rubbed at the tension in her shoulders, forcing a long sigh out of his lungs. Let it go, don't push, he told himself, and he smiled ruefully at the thought that it was far easier said than done these days, since this chronic case of responsibility had set in. A turbulent mix of emotions twisted inside him as he turned Alex and gazed down into her amber eyes.

"I love you," he whispered, bending his head down near hers.

"And I love you," Alex whispered back, rising up on the toes of her boots to kiss him. "Just don't try to run my life."

Standing at attention he clicked his heels together and gave her a smart salute and a dazzling smile. "I shall endeavor to do my best."

But the smile faded as he walked away, assailed by doubts.

"Do yourself a favor," Rylan grumbled as Christian reached the new barn and the row of box stalls that were draped in Quaid Farm blue. Christian's brows lifted. Ry shot a dark look at his wife, who stood holding their son's hand near the open door of Diamond Life's stall. "If you're going to get tangled up with a woman, make sure she's got sense enough to mind you."

"Too late for that," Christian muttered wryly.

His employer ignored him, wheeling instead to face his pregnant wife again with a thunderous black scowl. "You shouldn't be out in this heat, Mary Margaret."

"Oh, pooh, sugar." Maggie batted her lashes at him and patted her free hand to the crown of her wide-brimmed straw hat. "I've got my sunhat and my sundress on. I've got enough sunscreen to coat a horse with. Besides, I'm not a piece of wax fruit that's going to melt in the heat."

Christian bent and brushed a kiss to Maggie's expectantly upturned cheek and couldn't help but smile at her. "I think you look very fetching."

"Why, thank you," she said, preening as she let go of her son's hand and turned in a somewhat awkward circle, showing off her yellow dress and her enormous belly.

Ry snorted. "Yeah, we'll see how fetching she looks when we have to scrape her up off the ground after she passes out from the heat."

Maggie sent him a ferocious look.

"I expect Maggie knows her limits," Christian said without much conviction.

"She never has," Ry said flatly. "Why should she start now?"

Christian wasn't inclined to argue the point. He was in no position to. Hadn't he just finished trying to dissuade Alex from something she was bent on doing? He certainly didn't believe she knew her limits. Or maybe she did, he thought, frowning darkly as his suspicion came creeping back to him.

"Buddy Quaid, get out of that stall!" Ry barked, his fierce-eyed stare on his son, who had gone into the stall where the young stallion, Diamond Life, was being readied.

"But I was just gonna help Marlin," the boy said, frowning as his father scooped him up.

"You got to be taller to help Marlin," Ry explained, tucking the boy under his arm like a football.

"But I'm big," Buddy protested, looking at his father upside down. "I'm gonna be a big brother."

"Big brothers help their mamas," Katie Leone said, coming to stand beside her own big brother, who leaned down and kissed her dutifully. She tickled her nephew's chin and chuckled as he squealed and squirmed.

"How did the baby-sitting go?" Christian asked as he took Isabella from Nick's arms and rubbed noses with her. The baby immediately began regaling him with gibberish, her small hands waving as she spoke.

"Great," Nick said, pulling Katie backward into his embrace. "Isabella is an angel."

"Yes, she is, isn't she," Christian said, feeling ridiculously proud of the dark-eyed little girl, as if he were somehow responsible for her good behavior. As if he were her father. Gads, he thought, swallowing hard.

"Maybe you're the one who shouldn't go out in the heat, sugar," Maggie said, giving him a look that mixed humor and sympathy. "You're looking a might peaked."

The woman was too perceptive by half. He ignored her remark, turning instead to Katie and Nick. "Alex tells me you two are expecting, so to speak."

"We're on the list," Nick said with glowing brown eyes as he hugged his wife and grinned.

Katie looked more than a little nervous at the idea. "It could be a long wait," she said, fussing with the gathers in her pink gauze skirt.

"Well, congratulations anyway, luv," Christian said sincerely as he handed Isabella to her. "You'll be a wonderful mother."

Katie smiled and glanced away, blinking back sudden tears.

"We should maybe go find Alex, huh?" Nick suggested gently, steering her away. He glanced back over his shoulder at the others apologetically but managed a happy tone as he said, "Hey, dinner at our place after the show. My mama's special deep-dish pizza and plenty of cold stuff to wash it down."

"Was it something I said?" Christian murmured as he watched them walk away, Nick with his arm around Katie's shoulder and his dark head tilted down toward hers solicitously.

"She's just a little unsure of herself," Maggie said, her eyes full of concern.

Ry scowled as he set his son down. "And we all know whose fault that is."

"Rylan, let it go," Maggie said wearily, leaning against his oaklike frame. "Your mama ran out on you a long time ago. It's best left in the past."

"Yeah," he said reflectively, "but look how often the past comes back to haunt us."

Christian went into the stall to check on his horse, his mind wandering once again to Alex. If his suspicions were correct, it was her past that was driving her to take risks. How long would she allow it to haunt her? More important, could he stop her before she let it destroy her?

Charlie ran a cloth over the sorrel mare's glossy coat, then ran a different one over Alex's boots, removing every speck of mud from horse and rider in preparation for their appearance in the show ring. If they came out looking less than spotless, it would be through no fault of the groom.

"Make sure Heather C. keeps Rugby moving," Alex said, straightening her jacket and wincing at the feel of sweat running between her shoulder blades. "His back will tighten up if she just sits around on him gossiping."

"Don't you worry, miss. I'll crack the whip," Charlie said.

"And I'll want you here with him the instant I finish with Duchess."

"Right."

As she polished the visible edge of stirrup iron, the groom suddenly cast a suspicious glance over her shoulder and stiffened in affront.

"What the bloody hell do you want?" she barked. "A flaming lot of nerve you have, showing your face round here! Who do think you are?"

Alex's gaze was immediately pulled from the ring to the handsome man standing beside her horse wearing dark sunglasses and a sheepish expression. Robert Braddock. If Charlie's reception of the man had been fiery, Alex's was glacial. She stared down at him from her much greater height as if she were the queen of the world and he a filthy, traitorous pockmarked peasant.

He cleared his throat nervously and pulled his sunglasses off, revealing the remnants of a beastly hangover. "I wonder if I could have a word with you, Alex?"

"For what?" Charlie demanded. She cuffed Braddock on the arm and scolded him in a voice a decibel too shrill for his pounding head to stand. "Go on, you ruddy blighter! You've got nothing my miss wants to hear! We've all had a bellyful of you, we have. You ought to be ashamed—"

"I am," he admitted, giving her a determined look, his words stopping her arm in midswing as she hauled back to clip him another one.

They both glanced up to Alex for a sign. She nodded Charlie away. The girl took a reluctant step in the direction of the ring, shaking a warning finger at Braddock. "This had better be good, Bobby, mind you, or you'll have me to answer to. Right?"

"Gawd, she's something else," Braddock muttered, rubbing at his throbbing temples. "That girl could sell sass by the gallon and still have a surplus," he said, turning his patented good-ol'-boy grin up toward Alex.

"What did you want to say to me, Mr. Braddock?" Alex asked, freezing the charming smile right off his square face. The wounds that had been opened the night before were still too tender for her to be readily forgiving. "Please be brief, I have to ride soon."

"I want to apologize for last night," he said smoothly, going for endearing contrition, since charm had been knocked out of the box. He tilted his head and gave her a boyish smile. "I'm really sorry, Alex."

"And that makes it all right?" Alex asked, cold fury building inside her from the leftover ashes of another fight with a handsome, charming man who had believed his looks and his position allowed him to get away with anything. "I don't think so."

Braddock's bloodshot dark eyes flashed a little. His jaw hardened a fraction. His drawl had lost some of its honey when he spoke again. "I didn't mean any harm."

Alex stared at him, unblinking. "You made me the butt of a joke. You thought you could just play with my life for your own amusement."

"I said I was sorry." His patience was wearing thin in big patches now, his expression taking on a hard-ness Alex doubted he often let other people see. "You know, maybe if you'd been a little friendlier to begin with, none of this would have happened."

His tone and his words struck another raw nerve. "I'm sorry, Mr. Braddock," she said with frigid for-mality, "but I don't feel obligated to be 'friendly' to men who consider it their due."

With that Alex nudged her horse forward, buck-ling the strap of her helmet as she headed for the arena. As she cantered her mare in a slow circle she glanced out to see Robert Braddock glare at her, then turn on his booted heel and storm away. She'd made herself an enemy, but there was no time to dwell on it now.

By late afternoon everyone had abandoned their jackets to ride in shirtsleeves with the blessings of the judges. The heat had climbed another sweltering degree toward one hundred, and what little breeze there had been in the morning had died a stagnant death. The air hung damp and hazy over the thickly forested hillsides that rose around Green Hills.

"He's gonna tear 'em up today. Aren't you, big guy?" Tully boomed, slapping his hand against the wire grill of Terminator's stall.

The gelding was tacked up and tied to either side of the stall. He sat back on his haunches, wild-eyed, and lunged forward, jerking at his bonds.

Tully laughed and banged the stall again. "Just look at him. He's rearin' to go!"

"Mr. Haskell, please don't do that," Alex snapped impulsively grabbing hold of Tully's wrist as he started to hit the grill again.

The big man turned and looked down at her, a curious mix of anger and speculation on his meaty face.

Alex dropped his hand abruptly and stepped back. "We don't want him to leave his game in the locker room, do we?"

"No," Haskell said slowly, pulling out a handkerchief to dab at the sweat on his forehead.

Uncomfortable with his sudden close scrutiny, Alex moved away from him and bent to dig her gloves and crop out of her gear bag. She sincerely wished Tully Haskell would have been too caught up rubbing elbows with the rich and famous to bother checking up on her. Both she and Terminator were nervous enough as it was. The course for the grand prix was being set up. In a few moments the riders would be allowed to walk it, judging the distances, making strategy. Alex wanted no distractions.

"I see you haven't come to your senses yet," Christian said dryly.

She closed her eyes, loath to look up and see whether he was talking to her or Tully. This is all I need, she thought, for the two of them to get into it right here in Hill's stable. Lovely.

"Don't you have stalls to muck out, Atherton?" Tully asked caustically.

Christian gave the man a cool, dismissing look

and turned away from him, his focus on Alex. He'd watched her warm up Terminator. The rogue had done his best to run off with her. He'd fought her every step. And now he stood in his stall looking as if he were possessed by demons—rolling his eyes, grinding his teeth, kicking out with his hind legs. The horse looked insane, and the thought of Alex climbing back up on him drove Christian near that very same edge. His earlier promise of noninterference had gone by the wayside, thrown over by the suddenly dominant need to protect the woman he loved.

"Christian, we aren't going to discuss this," Alex said, struggling for an ounce of coolheadedness as she straightened.

"Don't be such a stubborn little fool, Alex!" he said, his temper flaring to rival the heat wave. Grabbing her arm he turned her toward the stall. "Look at him. The poor beast is completely off his head!"

"Butt out, Atherton," Tully said, shoving Christian back a step. "You charmed her into sleeping with you, but you can't charm her into losing to you."

"You bastard!" Christian spat the word, his British reserve evaporating in a haze of fury. He had taken all he intended to from this ill-mannered lout. He wasn't about to stand for Haskell making sleazy gossip of his love for Alex. Acting completely on instinct, he hauled his arm back and bloodied Haskell's nose with one forceful punch.

"Christian, stop it!" Alex shouted.

He dragged his eyes off Tully, who was swearing a muffled blue streak as he held his handkerchief to his nose and dyed it red with his own blood. Reason came seeping back into his brain as he looked down at Alex. She was furious with him. Her eyes blazed with golden light beneath ominously lowered black brows. Her chin had lifted to that foreboding angle he recognized all too well.

"I think you'd better go," she said.

"Alex, please—"

She held her hands up to ward off whatever explanation he had to offer. "Go. Now."

"Fine," he said, pulling himself together, straightening his back, setting his shoulders, lifting his aristocratic nose a fraction. Love had reduced him to a brawling bully. It had reduced him to begging. Who needed it? "Don't expect sympathy when that rogue throws you through a fence."

There were thirty horses entered in the Green Hills grand prix. Three had been scratched due to heat exhaustion. Terminator was not among them. Christian watched from atop Diamond Life as Alex tried to work the horse in a slow circle. The gelding refused to walk, dancing instead in a series of hops and leaps, his head way up, nostrils flaring. His coat was nearly black with sweat, white lather foaming along his neck and dripping from his mouth. Alex sat on him, her back rigid with the strain of holding the big horse in check, the muscles standing out in her arms. Christian's stomach churned.

"She deserves whatever happens to her, if you ask me," Robert grumbled, circling his gray around Christian's horse.

Christian shot him a dire look. "Nobody asked you."

Braddock swore under his breath. "What's the matter with you? Getting yourself all tied up in knots over a woman. It's not like you."

It might not have been like the Christian Atherton who had cavalierly bet his friend he could win a certain lady's favors, but it was very like the Christian Atherton who had evolved over the past few weeks. He had done a great deal of growing and changing in a short space of time. The pains of that growth were still stinging and aching through him, evident in the set of his square chin and the tension in his shoulders.

Braddock grinned. "Why don't I call us up a couple of first-stringers from my little black book? We'll head into DC tonight and take your mind off that razor-tongued little viper."

Christian gave him a look of utter disdain and moved his horse away. "Grow up, Robert."

He was as disgusted with himself as he was with his friend. He didn't enjoy the turbulent emotions warring inside him. He didn't like dealing with new feelings. He wasn't at all certain he would be any good at respectability. Just look what he'd done defending Alex's honor. Punching her client in the nose! She'd love him for that. Well, bloody hell, she deserved better than Tully Haskell, whether she believed it or not.

Wiping the sweat off his brow with his forearm, he tried to drag his concentration off Alex and back to the matter at hand. He had a jump course to ride.

A grand prix course is designed to challenge both horse and rider. The fences are imposing, the distances between them difficult. This course was no exception, and adding to the difficulty was the gooey top layer of footing in the ring. The heat and humidity would be a factor for horses who lacked stamina. Whoever went home with the lion's share of the prize money was going to have earned it. There would be no easy victories.

Christian set his young stallion to the task with his characteristic determination. He may have been easygoing outside the ring, but in it he was the consummate competitor. He attacked the course with a combination of aggression and finesse and a confidence that was telegraphed to the handsome equine star beneath him. They came away with a clear round.

Others were not so fortunate. Countless rails came down, particularly at a big triple bar with a deceptive curving approach. Several horses slipped turning corners. Two riders came off. By the time twenty had gone, there were only four clean rounds.

Alex waited her turn near the end gate, a terrible feeling of foreboding boring through her like acid. There was no way in hell Terminator was going to make it through this, and yet she felt she had no alternative but to try him. Driven by something that went way beyond the issue of job security, she rode the chestnut gelding into the ring. She had to prove herself. She had to pay her dues.

Wrestling for control of the bit, she took her horse into the first fence. He put an extra stride in at the last second, jumped badly, and rapped the top rail hard, but it stayed up. The instant his feet touched the ground, the battle was on again. He lunged against the bit, pulling Alex up out of the saddle. This time he left the ground too early, ignoring the signals of his rider, but jumped big and left the second fence intact.

The fight for control raged on. Alex's arms felt like hot lead from trying to hold Terminator to a manageable pace. Pain knifed into her shoulders and fear climbed high in her throat. Because Terminator refused to listen to her, he was out of position coming into nearly every fence, and as a consequence Alex was out of position. The horse made the jumps on sheer physical talent. She clung to him through pure athleticism.

They were coming into the toughest part of the course—a combination of three jumps with one stride between each followed by the curve into the triple bar. As they started for it, Terminator ducked his head again, jerking the reins through Alex's numb hands, which allowed him a burst of dangerous speed. By luck they made the first of the combination in perfect stride, but they hit the second one soundly, bringing down the top rail. Alex was thrown forward on landing, giving Terminator free rein as she struggled to stay aboard. He ducked out on the third fence of the combination and rounded the turn at breakneck pace for the triple bar.

Alex had taken falls before—as a seasoned rider, she expected to take her share of spills. But this wasn't just a tumble, it was a catastrophe. This was the kind of crash that ended careers, even lives.

Terminator galloped for the triple bar out of control, wild, running as if he were being chased by the devil himself. He cut the corner too sharply, saw the fence too late, tried to put on the brakes, and slipped in the mud, then took off in a last-ditch effort to save himself. He went up in the air, twisting as his hind legs slipped out from under him, and then went crashing down.

Alex saw it all happen in slow motion—the jerky takeoff, the sudden terrible change of angle, the red-and-white bars of the fence rushing up at her, then nothing.

When the blackness receded, she was looking up at half a dozen anxious faces. Her fuzzy gaze focused in on one.

"Christian?"

He was on his knees beside her, mud staining his immaculate white breeches, sweat running in rivers down his ashen face. His eyes were bright with an emotion like panic. "Lie still, darling," he said, his voice choked and hoarse. He ran a trembling hand back through her hair. "Just lie still. There's a doctor coming."

"I'm all right," she said, groaning as she struggled to sit up. "All right" was a gross exaggeration. She felt as if she'd been beaten with a club, but none of the pain was the kind associated with broken bones. She looked at him anxiously. "The horse?"

"Damn the horse!" Christian barked, his face flaming a furious shade of red.

The horse! If he'd had a gun, he would have shot the hateful creature there and then. Nothing, *nothing* in his life had ever terrified him the way seeing her fall had—watching Alex lose control, watching the horse go down in a tangle of legs and lumber. It had nearly killed him to see it happen, to fear the worst, to bend over Alex as she lay unconscious for those few terrible seconds. And she was asking about the bloody horse!

"The horse is fine Ms. Gianni," one of the ring stewards said from somewhere above her.

Alex nodded, wincing at the throbbing that set off in her head. Helmet or no, she'd taken quite a jolt. Still, she was in one piece and saw no reason not to demonstrate that fact to the five hundred people watching. Hanging on to Christian's arm for support, she pushed herself to her feet and was rewarded with a round of applause for her efforts.

An hour later she'd been thoroughly checked over by the doctor on call and pronounced whole and healthy. Half her body was liable to turn black and blue, and she had a nasty cut on her right cheekbone, but it wasn't anything she hadn't endured before.

She was sitting on a trunk in the stall where her tack was stored, holding a bag of ice to her cheek when Christian reappeared. After helping her from the ring to the ambulance and hovering like a mother hen while the doctor checked her for a concussion, he had been called back to the arena to ride in the jump-off.

"How'd it go?" she asked, trying to muster a smile that ended up looking more like a grimace.

"I blew the combination," he said flatly. "We came third."

"Oh."

She watched him pace the small enclosure with his hands on his hips. His head was bent, his pale hair falling onto his forehead. Nervous tension surrounded him like an electrical field. It beamed out of his blue eyes like lasers when he stopped and looked at her from under lowered brows. He was angry, she realized. Furious. The storm was being controlled by his proper British manners, but the manners were clearly in danger of losing their grip.

"You could have been killed," he said, breaking the silence that had become unbearable.

"But I wasn't."

The first explosion broke through his control like a thunderclap. "Dammit, Alex, that isn't the point!"

"We ride, we take risks, Christian," she said, maintaining her calm. "You know that. You take them too."

"Acceptable risks," he stipulated, jabbing the air between them with a slender forefinger. "There's a line there, and you've gone way across it, Alex."

"What are you saying?"

"I'm saying that this reckless disregard for your life has got to stop. You're shipping that horse back to Haskell immediately."

She bristled at his autocratic mind-your-betters tone of voice. "That's not for you to decide, Christian. You don't run my life."

The second rumble of thunder shook the rafters above them. "Well, somebody's got to, because you're bloody well going to kill yourself!"

"I'm just doing my job," Alex said tightly.

Christian shook his head. "This goes well beyond doing your job or hanging on to your damnable independence. You're trying to punish yourself. You think you have to take on the likes of that rogue to make up for all the imagined sins you committed in California, for all the things you lost—"

"That's absurd!" she exclaimed, vaulting off the tack trunk as if it had suddenly turned red-hot.

"It's self-destructive, Alex, and it's stupid—"

"It's a damned lie!" she shouted, her heart pounding wildly.

"Is it?" Christian demanded softly. His fingers closed around her chin and tilted her bruised face upward. "Look me in the eye, Alex. Look me in the eye and tell me you don't blame yourself for what that bastard Reidell did to you."

Tears and defiance rose in her eyes, but denial wouldn't come. She could feel the words stick in her throat like a rock, but she couldn't force them out. She glared at Christian, hating him for doing this to her, for making her feel things she didn't want to feel and face things she didn't want to face. Her own sense of fury built inside her, but all the words stayed bottled up, and the pressure built.

Christian sighed and slid his palm along her uninjured cheek.

"I love you, Alex," he murmured. "But I can't stand by and watch you break your neck in penance for something that wasn't your fault."

"What are you saying?"

"I'm saying that horse goes or I go," Christian said, gritting his teeth. He'd never been one for ultimatums. He'd never been one for manipulating people. But then he'd never been in love. Nor had he ever stood helplessly by while someone he loved risked her life and came close to losing it. He had to do something to save her, to save himself, and this was the only thing he could think of.

"I can't afford—"

"You can't afford not to. Think of Isabella if you can't think of yourself. What would have happened to her if you'd been killed or crippled out there today? And all for nothing, Alex!" he said plaintively. "I know money is a problem, but I can help you if you'll let me. You don't need Haskell." *You need me. Please say you need me.*

"I don't need to be bullied either," Alex said, striking out, old wounds stinging more sharply than the new. "And I don't need you psychoanalyzing me. You're blowing this all out of proportion because you've got some macho obsessive need to control my life. Well, I've got news for you, buster," she said, flinging the ice bag at him. It hit his shoulder and fell to the wooden floor of the stall. She kicked it aside as she moved to stand toe to toe with him. "I'm in control," she declared. "Nobody tells me what to do or who to be or how to dress," she said, her voice rising with each word. *"I'm in control!"*

The shout rang in her own ears, the volume and pitch making it painfully obvious that what she said was not true. She stared at Christian just the same, unwilling to back down. And he stared back, his handsome face carefully blank.

"You know where to find me," he said quietly,

using every ounce of strength he had to tamp down the pain ripping through his chest.

"Who says I'll come looking?" Alex was certain her words hurt her more than they hurt Christian. Her heart wrenched as she said them and he walked away, out of her stall and out of her life.

Eleven

It hurt to move. The slightest shift of weight set off small explosions of pain throughout the right side of her body. Her shoulder throbbed abominably. The muscles all down her side felt as though they'd been run through a meat grinder. Alex recognized the distinctive kinds of pain from each distinctive injury. She'd been hurt often enough to distinguish one from the next. There was the pain that came from torn muscle fibers. The pain that came from blood pooling beneath the surface of the skin. The pain that lingered from the jolt of a sudden, hard impact.

But the physical pain was a welcomed distraction from the emotional pain that permeated her entire being, so on Monday morning, at the crack of dawn, Alex inched her way out of bed and hobbled down the hall for a therapeutic soak in the tub. Rigid muscles let loose to some degree, at least until she was able to raise her right arm almost to shoulder height by the time she struggled out of the water twenty minutes later.

As she had expected, most of the right side of her body was purpling from the forceful landing on the thick wooden bars of the jump. Anything but the slightest brush of the towel made her wince, and every time she winced, the cut on her cheek tugged at the butterfly patch the doctor had applied. The pain in her cheek made her grit her teeth, and gritting her teeth amplified the pounding in her head.

"Face it, Gianni," she muttered to her battered reflection in the mirror. "You just can't win for losing."

She would have made a good extra for a horror movie. Cheap, too. There would have been no need for a makeup artist to make her look ghastly. In addition to the welts and bruises her fall had raised, she was pasty pale. The dark crescents under her eyes were a testimony to a night spent doing something other than sleeping.

Hurting had taken up the entire night. Hurting from the fall. Hurting worse from Christian's abdication. Hurting from loneliness. Hurting from self-doubt. Hurting from anger. There had seemed to be no escape from it as the night had stretched on, hot and relentless. And morning offered no respite. Every painful thought gave birth to another, creating a never-ending cycle of pain.

Struggling into her peach-colored robe and fumbling awkwardly with the belt, Alex hobbled out of the bathroom and down the hall to see the one person in her life who had yet to pass judgment on her.

Isabella sat in her crib carrying on a conversation with herself as she played with a yellow stuffed pony Christian had given her. Her attention snapped immediately to the door as Alex stepped in, and the baby grinned her father's endearing, crooked grin.

"Mama!"

"Hi, button," Alex whispered, managing to smile on only one side of her face as she crossed the room to lift her daughter out of the crib with her good arm. "Glad you recognized me. I don't think I could have stood it if you'd have started crying at the sight of me."

Isabella was more interested in the bandage on her mother's cheek than on what her mother had to say. Dark eyes intense, she reached out to poke her index finger at it, making Alex suck her breath in through her teeth.

"No-no, sweetie. That hurts Mama."

"No no no no no," Isabella babbled, shaking her head emphatically, her dark curls bouncing.

Alex smiled and rubbed her daughter's nose with the tip of her own. "Hey, you, keep the racket down. You'll wake Pearl. She'll go back to her niece and leave us to fend for ourselves if we don't watch out."

Isabella giggled, delighted by her mother's expression if not her words.

They went through their regular morning routine at the changing table—a fresh diaper, a liberal dusting of powder to combat the sweltering heat, brushing the baby's thick hair and pinning it off her neck and away from her face with half a dozen minuscule barrettes. Alex moved much more slowly and clumsily than usual, but she had no intention of giving up this time with her daughter. Isabella was the one constant thing in her life, the one person who loved her unconditionally. This morning in particular Alex felt the need to take comfort in those basic truths. This morning when she felt so alone.

What a difference a day could make, she thought. Yesterday she had awakened in Christian's arms, the warm magic of his lips drawing her up out of the depths of sleep. They had made love as the sun rose, neither of them saying a word, just watching each other's eyes as their bodies communicated the love that was in their hearts. This morning he was on the other side of the hill, going about his life, and she was there aching, feeling adrift and uncertain and alone, as if she'd been abandoned for a hundred years.

"I miss him," she admitted in a tight whisper.

Her left hand fumbled with Isabella's little duckie hairbrush, and the tears she had managed to hold at bay all night sprang up suddenly to fill her eyes. Saying the words aloud had opened the floodgates she had fought to keep bolted shut. Now the whole complement of marauding emotions rushed to assault her, all of them expressed in one torturous word that seemed to reverberate through her chest—*why.*

Why did he have to be so demanding? Why did she have to be so stubborn? Why did life have to kick her every time she thought she finally had it by the tail? And why did it have to hurt so damn much?

"Alex! What are you doing out of bed?" Pearl demanded, bustling into the room. She was already dressed in spite of the fact that it was not yet seven o'clock. A sensible cotton shift flowed shapelessly over her pudgy frame. Her frizz of steel gray hair was combed. Pearl maintained that she had risen at six-thirty for sixty-some years, and retirement was no reason to break a perfectly good habit.

"I'm better off moving around," Alex said, mentally wincing at the hoarseness in her voice. She kept her back to her housemate, trying to erase discreetly any remnants of the tears that had threatened. "Trust me. I've been through this before. It only hurts when I laugh."

"Doesn't look like you've been doing much of that," the older woman observed sagely as she scooped up Isabella from the changing table and perched her on one plump hip.

Nor am I likely to, Alex thought grimly.

"I've got two good ears," Pearl said. "And there ain't nothing they haven't heard at least once already. So if you feel like talking, honey, you just go right on ahead."

Once she would have accepted the offer eagerly, but Alex had since taught herself to keep her own counsel. Too many confidants had been disappointed and disapproving. Still, she appreciated Pearl's offer and mustered a half-smile for it. "Thanks, Pearl, but I'll be all right."

The woman frowned. "Only the good Lord can handle everything by himself, girl, and you're not the Almighty. You'd best remember that." Clucking to herself, she bustled out of the room, bouncing Isabella in her arms as she went.

Alex hobbled to her room to dress. It was already sweltering in the little cubicle. The old fan in the window groaned and rattled, threatening death due to overwork. Alex stripped off her robe and caught what little breeze the thing made, thinking it might be her last chance to do so before it gave out altogether. She stared at the image of herself in the mirror above the dresser, taking in the cropped hair, the gaunt cheeks, the haunted eyes. And she remembered the girl with the long, wild mane and the flashing, tempestuous smile. The woman who stared back at her looked like a prisoner. A prisoner of the past. A prisoner of the ideas that had taken root in her mind during that horrible time after the rape.

You're too forward, Alexa.

You've always been so flirtatious.

You were asking for it.

It was your own fault.

And joining in that chorus from the past came Christian's voice. *You're punishing yourself.*

Was she?

Her good hand lifted to her boyish short hair and fingered the ends absently as a strange sense of panic slid through her.

Suddenly she jerked her hand away and put on the mental brakes. No, she wasn't trying to punish herself. She wasn't doing anything destructive. She was just trying to make a living. No one had ever said it should be easy or without risks. She had to pay her dues.

Pay your dues for what?

She pressed a hand to her belly as that chilling, sliding sensation dropped through her stomach again. Swearing in Italian, she turned from the mirror and limped to the closet. Refusing to sink any further into depression, she fumbled into a pair of jeans and a loose, sleeveless blue work shirt and made her way down to the barn, where Charlie had already begun morning chores.

"Blimey, miss! You hadn't ought to be down here!" the girl protested as she scooped oats out of the feed cart and dumped them into the box of the roan anxiously awaiting his breakfast. A chorus of nickers sounded down the row from the still hungry. Charlie ignored their pleas and stared indignantly at Alex, as if her being there was somehow insulting.

Alex frowned. "Everyone seems to know what's best for me."

"Well, it's a cinch you don't," Charlie said with typical bluntness. "You couldn't ride a bicycle, the shape you're in, let alone a horse!"

"I'll agree with you there. No reason I can't do the grooming, though, while you muck out the stalls."

"Oh, right," the groom said sarcastically. "No reason a'tall. It's not like you just got yourself chucked off into a fence and half-fallen on by that ugly great moose of an animal."

They both looked across the aisle at Terminator, who was weaving in his stall with his ears pinned, looking angry at the world.

"The work will do me good," Alex said.

"I'm sure," Charlie said with a rude snort. She shook her head in reproach, wiping the sweat from her forehead up into the hedge of burgundy hair that defied even the most wilting humidity. "A right flaming twit, you are."

Alex watched the girl move off down the aisle muttering under her breath and shaking her head in utter disgust. She wondered briefly what she was going to do about Charlie, then wondered miserably what she was going to do without her. She had grown terribly fond of the sassy groom, but she couldn't allow Christian to go on paying Charlie's wages, and she couldn't afford to pay them herself. The van needed repairs, and Terminator had managed to destroy her best saddle in the fall. Those two things were priorities. Hired help was a luxury.

Some people found solace in music, some in gardening, some in prayer. Alex had always found hers in the methodical work of brushing a horse. Her mind was free to comtemplate as her hands stroked the various brushes over the coat of the animal, working out the dust and bringing a lustrous shine to the hair. Today she found no real peace. The task itself was painful and difficult, and her mind was bent on dredging up anger and excuses instead of sorting through all that for calmer emotions.

She was sick of people telling her what to do and how to do it. She was sick of people analyzing her at every turn. She had come there to rebuild her life, and that was what she was going to do. So she had gotten hurt in the process—it was a dangerous business. She'd known Terminator wasn't ready for that course. The only mistake she'd made had been in not insisting they pull him from the competition. The horse just needed some time and understanding. He'd come around.

"Get away from me, you son of a dog!" Charlie's voice rang out, fierce and panicked. It was followed by the snort of a horse, the sharp pounding sound of hooves striking wood, and then a cry.

Heart in her throat, Alex dropped her brush and hurried down the aisle, blocking her own injuries from her mind. The wheelbarrow stood by Terminator's door, and she could see the big gelding whirling and lunging in the stall, his ears flat to his head. Her blood ran cold as she realized she couldn't see the groom.

"Charlie!" she yelled, flinging the stall door back.

The girl lay in the straw, huddled into a fetal position with her hands over her head and her back against the wall. Blood ran freely from a cut on one forearm. The horse wheeled and lunged toward her again.

Pain exploding through her own body, Alex grabbed up the pitchfork and swung it like a baseball bat, catching Terminator hard across the chest and startling him into retreat. He stood at the back of the stall, snorting and rearing, his eyes rolling wildly in his head.

Straining to hold the pitchfork up with her right arm, Alex inched her way into the stall and squatted down next to the fallen groom. "Charlie, can you hear me? Are you conscious?"

"Bloody hell," the girl said, sobbing. "I wish I weren't. The bastard broke me arm."

"Can you move? I don't know if I can drag you."

Crying and cursing, Charlie struggled to her knees and crawled out of the stall while Alex fended Terminator off with the fork.

They drove to the emergency room in Briarwood in grim silence, Charlie caught up in trying to ward off the pain, Alex plunged into a black depression that didn't lessen even two hours later when the girl's arm had been set and she had been given permission to leave the hospital.

"It weren't your fault, miss," Charlie mumbled as Alex piloted her old car back toward the farm. Painkillers had dulled her senses. She leaned back against the torn upholstery and gazed down at the pristine plaster cast on her arm. "It weren't your fault a'tall."

Alex said nothing.

When she had Charlie settled in the house, she went back down to the barn and stood in front of Terminator's stall.

It *was* her fault. She'd known all along the horse was dangerous. Why, then, had she kept him? Her gaze drifted to the next stall where Duchess stood quietly munching hay, and she knew that Christian was right. This didn't really have anything to do with the mare. She had told herself it did, because that had been a convenient and viable excuse—but it wasn't the truth.

When she looked deep inside herself, past logic and rationalization, past all the defenses she brandished like a warrior's shield, there lay the fear that she had somehow brought all her troubles down on her own head, that she was to blame and now she had to earn back everything she'd lost.

Maybe Christian was right. Maybe those fears had driven her to take the kind of risks she had with Terminator.

Despite the choking heat Alex shivered at the thought. Why hadn't she seen it? Why hadn't she realized how stupid she was being, how stubborn? Why hadn't she seen what her past had driven her to? It was self-destructive and irresponsible. Now Charlie lay with a broken arm because of her. The girl might have been killed. She thought of the fall she'd taken and all the other injuries this animal had inflicted on her. She might have been killed, and for what? Because she had seen a need to punish herself.

"*Madre di Dio*," she whispered, pressing a hand across her eyes as misery spread through her.

What had she become? What had she allowed Greg Reidell to turn her into? The rape had destroyed her life, shattered her support network, driven her to an obsessive need for self-reliance and a destructive need to punish herself. And now someone else had been endangered because of it. How long was she going to let Greg Reidell go on raping her life?

"Enough," she whispered as she backed away from the stall. She was all through being a victim.

Feeling old and tired Alex went into the tack room and used the phone there to call Tully Haskell. She left a message on his answering machine asking him to stop by. Then she went back to her grooming and her thinking, letting her mind work on the best way to get Christian back.

Christian sat on the fence of the outdoor arena, staring off at the rolling pastures of Quaid Farm, feeling an odd sort of detachment. This was the only home he had ever known in the States. In many ways it had been more of a home to him than Westerleigh Manor ever had. But the sense of comfort and contentment he had always known here had drifted away. There was a restlessness inside him, a yearning that had been stirred to life by a tempestuous, amber-eyed minx. He suddenly found himself wanting all the things he had shied away from his whole life—ties, responsibilities, a wife, children.

Poor Uncle Dicky, he thought with a fond, sad

smile, the last of the Atherton black sheep has gone respectable.

The storm of emotions that had raged inside him had played itself out. He felt calm, accepting of his fate. The role of bachelor rake could fall on some younger buck's shoulders. Christian Atherton was ready for other, more important things.

The question was: How to convince Alex? In many ways she was as untamable as that horse she rode, fiery and spirited and full of distrust. He smiled at the thought. He was going to have his hands full trying to handle her, but he knew how sweet and loving she could be, how responsive she was to a gentle touch, how tender was her heart.

He ached with missing her. Walking out of that stall had been one of the hardest things he'd ever done. All night long he'd lain awake in his empty bed feeling as if a huge chunk had been snatched out of his life. And he'd known a fear that had chilled him to the bone.

Alex was so bloody stubborn, so full of pride— what if she never gave in? What if his speculation had hit too close to the truth? She might choose to distance herself from him, thinking it too uncomfortable to be around someone who knew all her deepest secrets and vulnerabilities.

He simply couldn't let that happen.

He'd never been so consumed by a woman, so intrigued by all the facets that made up her complex personality. He was going to enjoy her riddles and mysteries for the rest of his life—provided he could make it over that final barrier of Alex's stubborn pride.

Confidence welled inside him as he hopped down from the fence and started across the dusty ring. There hadn't been a fence built that Christian Atherton couldn't jump.

Alex shut the stall door and leaned back against it with a sigh. The grooming was finished. The stalls were going to have to wait until her students came out in the evening. She simply couldn't manage the task herself. She felt as if she didn't have a bone left in her body. They had all melted down into the puddle of dull pain washing through her.

Picking up her bottle of mineral water from the floor, she took a swig, then poured the rest of it down over her head, letting it cool her and wash some of the dirt and sweat away.

"Mighty hot, ain't it?"

Gasping, Alex started back against the stall door. Staring at the open end of the barn, it took her eyes a moment to adjust to the bright sun that backlit the tall, bulky man. Her pulse raced, then slowed again. "Mr. Haskell, you startled me."

"Don't know why," Tully said smoothly, his boot heels clicking on the concrete as he ambled down the aisle. His yellow western shirt was sweat stained in big patches, and his fleshy face was red and shiny from the heat. His big nose looked mushy and swollen from the blow Christian had delivered. As he drew close, his squinting eyes followed the water stain that soaked into Alex's cotton work shirt, plastering it to her chest. "You called me."

"Yes, I did." She straightened away from the stall, plucking the damp fabric from her skin and clutching it in her fist. Dammit, when would she stop being so nervous in this man's company? Probably never, but then she doubted she would be seeing much of him after today.

"I thought you might," he admitted.

"Well, then, you know what I'm going to say."

"Got a pretty good idea," he said, his mouth twisting into a slow smile. "I was there yesterday when you sent Atherton packing. I was wondering how long it'd take for you to get sick of that British prig."

Alex frowned, unease sifting through her. "Mr. Haskell, I don't see what this has to do with my reason for calling you."

"You don't have to be coy with me, Alex. I know all about you."

Those last five words shot ice through her veins. She looked up at Haskell, praying to God she had misunderstood him.

"I know what kind of woman you are," he said, stepping a little closer, his gaze raking over her in a way that made her skin crawl. "I know what you need, what you're after."

"I don't know what you're talking about." The denial came almost as automatically as the need to step away, to put some distance between herself and the man towering over her.

"Sure you do, honey," Haskell insisted, his voice low and too friendly. Unperturbed by her retreat, he turned and followed her as she backed toward the tack room. "Doesn't the name Reidell ring a bell?"

Another bolt of cold electricity jolted through Alex. She took another jerky step backward.

"Ol' Jack and I have some mutual business interests," Tully went on, his smile growing lascivious. "He told me all about you, darlin'."

Alex felt her fear pool in her throat to choke her. She had been almost ready to let her guard down, to believe that no one around there knew or cared about her past. Now Tully Haskell was saying he'd known all along. The idea made her stomach turn. How many times had he looked at her, touched her, thinking heaven knew what?

"I know where Jack made his mistake," he said. "He should have paid you off and kept you at Wide Acre. You'd have done that snotty kid of his some good."

"It wasn't like that," Alex said in one desperate effort to make him understand. But Tully Haskell was no more interested in listening to her than anyone else had been. She could see by the feral gleam in his eyes that Reidell had told him the worst version of the story and he had eagerly believed it.

"Don't worry," he said, backing her up against the wall beside the tack-room door. "I won't make the same mistake. I'll take care of you, honey," he said, his voice dropping as his gaze settled on her mouth, "and you'll take care of me."

"No!" Alex shouted as Haskell lowered his head and tried to kiss her. She dodged his mouth, bringing her knee up hard into his groin.

Tully grunted and staggered back, his face turning burgundy as he clutched himself. "You little bitch!"

Alex turned to run, but he lunged out and caught her, his fingers digging brutally into her injured arm. The pain came in a wave that knocked her to her knees and dimmed her vision. Haskell's hands closed on her shoulders, and he dragged her back toward the tack room.

Alex let her body go limp, and for one blissful second unconsciousness beckoned, but Haskell's voice drew her back.

"Think you're too good for me, don't you? You'll only spread your legs for men like Reidell and Atherton because of their high-and-mighty names. Well, I've got news for you, sweetheart, you'll do it for me, and you'll damn well like it."

Galvanized into action, Alex jerked against his hold, her feet scrambling to make contact with the floor. He loosened his grip for an instant, and she bolted, only to be hauled back against him in a crushing bear hug. The smell of sweat and cigars choked her, and as she gasped for air, he tightened his embrace against her bruised ribs. She couldn't help but cry out, not only at the pain to her already-abused body, but at the injustice. She had done nothing to deserve this. Nothing at all.

Christian turned his car in at the end of Alex's drive, frowning at the sight of Tully Haskell's pickup parked at the end of the barn. The insufferable swine. He hadn't even bothered to come to the ambulance after Alex had fallen with his horse. The man was simply going to have to leave—now and forever. And Christian didn't much care how forceful he had to be in getting that message across. He didn't like the way Tully Haskell looked at Alex. The thought of him getting anywhere near her made him absolutely blind with jealous fury.

The cry that came from the dark interior of the stables as Christian climbed out of the Mercedes went through his heart like a knife. He ran for the barn, skidding to a startled halt at the sight that greeted him—Tully Haskell trying to force Alex into the tack room.

As Haskell turned his head to squint at the intruder, Alex managed to get one arm free. Her hand grabbed the first thing it found—a bridle hanging on a hook beside the door. Twisting around as best she could, she swung her weapon, and the heavy metal bit smashed into the side of Tully's face. Then they all went crashing to the ground as Christian hit Haskell at a run.

Alex rolled to the side and managed to pull herself up along the wall, gasping for air and wincing at the pain racking her body. Half doubled over, she watched as Christian hauled her attacker to his feet and hit him with a solid right to the stomach and a left to the jaw. Tully swayed on his feet. He managed to take one wild swing at Christian's head, but Christian blocked it and bloodied Haskell's nose for the second time in two days. This time the resounding crack of breaking bone went through the stable like a gunshot. Tully went down on his knees, blood running through his fingers as he pressed his hands to his face.

"Get up!" Christian demanded, his fists still curled in front of him. "Get up, you bastard, and let me finish the job!"

He spun around as Alex laid her hand on his arm. The adrenaline was humming through him. He'd never felt so furious or so primitive or so ready to kill. His cool veneer of sophistication had fallen completely away in the instant he'd realized Haskell's intent.

"I'll call the sheriff," Alex said, her voice trembling

so badly, she could manage nothing more than a whisper. She looked up at Christian, at the tautness of his face, the fierce intensity in his eyes, and a shiver went through her. "Let him deal with it."

Christian glanced back down at the man bleeding all over the concrete floor, and disgust coiled inside him like a snake. "Let's wait outside," he said, wrapping an arm around Alex's shoulders and steering her toward the door. "I can't stand the sight of him."

"Are you sure you're all right?" Christian asked again as he parked the Mercedes at the end of the barn.

Haskell's pickup was gone, having been driven into Briarwood by a deputy. They'd made a queer little motorcade winding down out of the hills to the quaint little college town—a sheriff's car, a truck, and a Mercedes, all of them headed for the courthouse. It hadn't been a pleasant experience, walking up the wide steps with the eyes of the curious following them. Nor had what followed been enjoyable. Christian had watched Alex give her statement as calmly as she could. He'd watched her fight back the tears and the fresh memory of what had happened to her, and it had made him thirst for Haskell's blood all over again.

That a man could treat a woman with such contempt, with such violence, sickened him. And to think that Alex had suffered through it all before, that she had suffered through it under the weight of disbelief and suspicion, tore him apart inside. He had never hurt for another person before in quite the same way. He had always considered himself compassionate, but only so far as his selfishness would allow. His own needs had come first. That was no longer the case.

"I'm better than I would have been if you hadn't shown up," Alex said, trying in vain to lighten the mood. She felt on the brink of shattering as she climbed out of the sports car and leaned back against the roof, stiff and trembling as she watched Christian round the front of the car.

"My God, Alex," he whispered, his voice strained.

He pulled her gently into his arms, careful of how he handled her. He needed to hold her, to reassure himself that he had indeed gotten there in time. If he'd had any reservations left about wanting to be responsible for another person, they had vaporized the instant he'd seen Alex struggling to get free of the man who would have raped her. He wanted never to let her out of his sight again, never to let her out of his arms again.

"I could have killed him for putting his hands on you."

"Me too," Alex said, tears fighting their way out of her tightly closed eyes and soaking into Christian's torn blue T-shirt. She let them come for a minute, let some of the pressure release. It seemed all right now that they were away from watchful eyes.

There was a peacefulness about the yard now. The sun had slid past its hottest point. A breeze stirred down through the woods, bringing a breath of fresh air and the lush scent of the forest. The calm of early evening hung around them, and Alex tried to absorb some of it into her, but she felt too dirty and too battered to accomplish it. Her skin crawled at the memory of what had happened and what had nearly happened.

"I hate that he touched me!" She snarled the words through her teeth, angry at the liberty Haskell had taken, at her inability to stop him, at the knowledge that the memory of those moments would stay with her forever.

"He won't touch you again, darling. We'll see to that."

Alex shuddered at the thought of another trial. Memories of the last one were too fresh in her mind—the humiliation, the futility of fighting on her own, the broken faith of the people she had needed most. She couldn't go through that again.

Christian easily read her mind. "I'll be right there

with you, love. I'll be beside you every step of the way." Bending his head down, he pressed a kiss to her temple.

"Ouch."

Christian jerked back and sent her an accusatory look. "You *are* hurt."

"So are you," Alex pointed out, sniffing back the tears.

She raised her good arm and brushed a fingertip against an abrasion on his left cheekbone. He winced. Stepping back, she looked him over for further damage. Both knees had torn out of his faded jeans. There was blood splattered on his blue T-shirt, but it wasn't his. His knuckles were raw where they had connected with Tully Haskell's face.

Her own blouse had torn at one shoulder, and her jeans were dirty. Blood from a scrape on her knee had soaked a stain through the denim. "We should go to the house. Pearl will put some antiseptic on those scrapes for you. She's thinking of turning the place into an infirmary."

"In a minute. We need to talk."

Alex tried to muster a nervous smile. "It can't wait until we're more presentable?"

"It's waited long enough already."

Taking her by the hand, he led her to the simple wooden bench that sat along the end of the barn and motioned for her to sit down. Alex lowered herself gingerly, her eyes on Christian as he paced back and forth in front of her. He looked like a man with a mission. Her heart pounded as she wondered whether that mission was good or bad.

In her mind there was a good chance that he would bow out of her life. Look what she'd embroiled him in! He had come looking for a woman to date, to have a few laughs with, and instead had gotten caught up in the web of her past, a past that showed no signs of fading away.

Finally, Christian stopped and turned to stare down at her, his eyes bluer than the summer sky above them. There was a tension in his chest that made breathing painful. He knew this was probably not the time or the place. He would have preferred a romantic setting. But what they had been through in the last twenty-four hours had shaken him to the core and spurred him now to say what was in his heart.

"I love you, Alex. Everything I said yesterday still holds true, but the fact of the matter is, I can't stand to be away from you. I love you, and I want you to be my wife."

He said it as if he expected her to put up a fight. Alex blinked at him, stunned.

"I want us to get married, buy a place of our own, and have a dozen children."

He stared at her again, waiting for a rebuttal like a disputatious debate-team captain.

"Sounds like you've got it all planned out," Alex said, watching him closely, awestruck by the determination that rolled off him like steam. People said clothes made the man, but even in tattered jeans Christian's powerful personality radiated around him like an aura.

He ran a hand back through his hair and set his jaw at a stubborn angle. "I know you don't want me trying to run your life, but you're wrong, Alex. I do have a right to say whether or not you should take risks. Loving you gives me that right, because it's no longer only your life you're risking, it's mine as well. Our lives are intertwined, now and forever, if I have anything to say about it. You may not like it, but there you have it."

Alex sat for a long minute staring down at the road as cars drove past. She had come to Virginia thinking she would have no one to rely on but herself. The idea of a relationship had seemed remote, nonexistent really. Now this magnificent man was towering over her telling her he wanted her to be his wife. This untamable rake who had collected hearts all over the Western world was asking her to marry him.

"I—I don't know what to say," she murmured, her

brows knitting in confusion as emotions swirled inside her like a tempest.

"Say you love me," Christian whispered, his heart in his throat. He dropped to his knees in front of her, gritting his teeth as gravel bit into his scraped skin.

Alex caught her breath at the sudden vulnerability in his expression. How could he doubt she loved him? Her heart ached from loving him. "I do love you."

"Then say you'll marry me." He hung on her silence, dying a little bit with every second that passed.

"I—I'm scared, Christian," Alex said at last, the words tumbling out as the realization struck her.

Too many good things had gone bad on her. Too many dreams had ended in disappointment. Christian knelt before her, golden and tempting, too good to be true. She trembled from the desire to embrace him and from the fear that he would somehow vanish from her grasp as so many other things dear to her had.

"I'm scared."

Christian took her hands in his. "Don't be afraid to reach out for happiness, Alex. You deserve it. You deserve to be loved and cherished. Don't deny yourself any longer because of the past. We have a future ahead of us."

He was right. She'd let her past wield too much power over her. She'd paid penance for it and suffered and cried. It was time to let go, to put it all behind her and look to the future, a future with a man she loved, a man who believed in her.

Christian watched as a slow smile curved Alex's lush mouth, and her eyes lit up with gold. He could actually feel his heart warm and expand in response. Leaning forward, he captured her smile with a tender kiss.

"Let's go see Dr. Pearl," he said, rising and drawing Alex up with him.

He draped an arm around her and held her close

as they started toward the old farmhouse, toward their new life.

And in his heart of hearts he said, *Good-bye, Uncle Dicky, wherever you are.*

THE EDITOR'S CORNER

As you look forward to the holiday season—the most romantic season of all—you can plan on enjoying some of the very best love stories of the year from LOVESWEPT. Our authors know that not all gifts come in boxes wrapped in pretty paper and tied with bows. In fact, the most special gifts are the gifts that come from the heart, and in each of the six LOVESWEPTs next month, characters are presented with unique gifts that transform their lives through love.

Whenever we publish an Iris Johansen love story, it's an event! In **AN UNEXPECTED SONG**, LOVESWEPT #438, Iris's hero, Jason Hayes, is mesmerized by the lovely voice of singer Daisy Justine and realizes instantly that she was born to sing his music. But Daisy has obligations that mean more to her than fame and fortune. She desperately wants the role he offers, but even more she wants to be touched, devoured by the tormented man who tangled his fingers in her hair. Jason bestows upon Daisy the gift of music from his soul, and in turn she vows to capture his heart and free him from the darkness where he's lived for so long. This hauntingly beautiful story is a true treat for all lovers of romance from one of the genre's premier authors.

In **SATURDAY MORNINGS**, LOVESWEPT #439, Peggy Webb deals with a different kind of gift, the gift of belonging. To all observers, heroine Margaret Leigh Jones is a proper, straitlaced librarian who seems content with her life—until she meets outrageous rogue Andrew McGill when she brings him her poodle to train. Then she wishes she knew how to flirt instead of how to blush! And Andrew's

(continued)

peaceful Saturday mornings are never the same after Margaret Leigh learns a shocking family secret that sends her out looking for trouble and for ways to hone her womanly wiles. All of Andrew's possessive, protective instincts rush to the fore as he falls head over heels for this crazy, vulnerable woman who tries just a bit too hard to be brazen. Through Andrew's love Margaret Leigh finally sees the error of her ways and finds the answer to the questions of who she really is and where she belongs—as Andrew's soul mate, sharing his Saturday mornings forever.

Wonderful storyteller Lori Copeland returns next month with another lighthearted romp, **'TIZ THE SEASON,** LOVESWEPT #440. Hero Cody Benderman has a tough job ahead of him in convincing Darby Piper that it's time for her to fall in love. The serious spitfire of an attorney won't budge an inch at first, when the undeniably tall, dark, and handsome construction foreman attempts to turn her orderly life into chaos by wrestling with her in the snow, tickling her breathless beside a crackling fire—and erecting a giant holiday display that has Darby's clients up in arms. But Darby gradually succumbs to Cody's charm, and she realizes he's given her a true gift of love—the gift of discovering the simple joys in life and taking the time to appreciate them. She knows she'll never stop loving or appreciating Cody!

LOVESWEPT #441 by Terry Lawrence is a sensuously charged story of **UNFINISHED PASSION.** Marcie Courville and Ray Crane meet again as jurors on the same case, but much has changed in the ten years since the ruggedly sexy construction worker had awakened the desire of the pretty, privi-

(continued)

leged young woman. In the intimate quarters of the jury room, each feels the sparks that still crackle between them, and each reacts differently. Ray knows he can still make Marcie burn with desire—and now he has so much more to offer her. Marcie knows she made the biggest mistake of her life when she broke Ray's heart all those years ago. But how can she erase the past? Through his love for her, Ray is able to give Marcie a precious gift—the gift of rectifying the past—and Marcie is able to restore the pride of the first man she ever loved, the only man she ever loved. Rest assured there's no unfinished passion between these two when the happy ending comes!

Gail Douglas makes a universal dream come true in **IT HAD TO BE YOU,** LOVESWEPT #442. Haven't you ever dreamed of falling in love aboard a luxury cruise ship? I can't think of a more romantic setting than the *QE2.* For Mike Harris it's love at first sight when he spots beautiful nymph Caitlin Grant on the dock. With her endless legs and sea-green eyes, Caitlin is his male fantasy come true—and he intends to make the most of their week together at sea. For Caitlin the gorgeous stranger in the Armani suit seems to be a perfect candidate for a shipboard romance. But how can she ever hope for more with a successful doctor who will never be able to understand her wanderer's spirit and the joy she derives from taking life as it comes? Caitlin believes she is following her heart's desire by traveling and experiencing life to the fullest—until her love for Mike makes her realize her true desire. He gives her restless heart the gift of a permanent home in his arms—and she promises to stay forever.

(continued)

Come along for the ride as psychologist Maya Stephens draws Wick McCall under her spell in **DEEPER AND DEEPER,** LOVESWEPT #443, by Jan Hudson. The sultry-eyed enchantress who conducts the no-smoking seminar has a voice that pours over Wick like warm honey, but the daredevil adventurer can't convince the teacher to date a younger man. Maya spends her days helping others overcome their problems, but she harbors secret terrors of her own. When Wick challenges her to surrender to the wildness beneath the cool facade she presents to the world, she does, reveling in his sizzling caresses and drowning in the depths of his tawny-gold eyes. For the first time in her life Maya is able to truly give of herself to another—not as a teacher to a student, but as a woman to a man, a lover to her partner—and she has Wick to thank for that. He's shown her it's possible to love and not lose, and to give everything she has and not feel empty inside, only fulfilled.

Enjoy next month's selection of LOVESWEPTs, while you contemplate what special gifts from the heart you'll present to those you love this season!

Sincerely,

Susann Brailey

Susann Brailey
Editor
LOVESWEPT
Bantam Books
666 Fifth Avenue
New York, NY 10103

FOREVER LOVESWEPT

SPECIAL KEEPSAKE
EDITION OFFER
$12⁹⁵
VALUE

Here's your chance to receive a special hardcover Loveswept "Keepsake Edition" to keep close to your heart forever. Collect hearts (shown on next page) found in the back of Loveswepts #426-#449 (on sale from September 1990 through December 1990). Once you have collected a total of 15 hearts, fill out the coupon and selection form on the next page (no photocopies or hand drawn facsimiles will be accepted) and mail to: Loveswept Keepsake, P.O. Box 9014, Bohemia, NY 11716.

FOREVER LOVESWEPT
SPECIAL KEEPSAKE EDITION OFFER
SELECTION FORM

Choose from these special Loveswepts by your favorite authors. Please write a 1 next to your first choice, a 2 next to your second choice. Loveswept will honor your preference as inventory allows.

Loveswept®

_____BAD FOR EACH OTHER   Billie Green

_____NOTORIOUS   Iris Johansen

_____WILD CHILD   Suzanne Forster

_____A WHOLE NEW LIGHT   Sandra Brown

_____HOT TOUCH   Deborah Smith

_____ONCE UPON A TIME...GOLDEN
       THREADS   Kay Hooper

Attached are 15 hearts and the selection form which indicates my choices for my special hardcover Loveswept "Keepsake Edition." Please mail my book to:

NAME:_____

ADDRESS:_____

CITY/STATE:_____ ZIP:_____

Offer open only to residents of the United States, Puerto Rico and Canada. Void where prohibited, taxed, or restricted. Allow 6 - 8 weeks after receipt of coupons for delivery. Offer expires January 15, 1991. You will receive your first choice as inventory allows; if that book is no longer available, you'll receive your second choice, etc.

THE SHAMROCK TRINITY

☐ **21975 RAFE, THE MAVERICK**
   by Kay Hooper $2.95

☐ **21976 YORK, THE RENEGADE**
   by Iris Johansen $2.95

☐ **21977 BURKE, THE KINGPIN**
   by Fayrene Preston $2.95

THE LATEST IN BOOKS
AND AUDIO CASSETTES

Paperbacks

☐	28416	**RIGHTFULLY MINE** Doris Mortman	$5.95
☐	27032	**FIRST BORN** Doris Mortman	$4.95
☐	27283	**BRAZEN VIRTUE** Nora Roberts	$4.50
☐	25891	**THE TWO MRS. GRENVILLES** Dominick Dunne	$4.95
☐	27891	**PEOPLE LIKE US** Dominick Dunne	$4.95
☐	27260	**WILD SWAN** Celeste De Blasis	$4.95
☐	25692	**SWAN'S CHANCE** Celeste De Blasis	$4.95
☐	26543	**ACT OF WILL** Barbara Taylor Bradford	$5.95
☐	27790	**A WOMAN OF SUBSTANCE** Barbara Taylor Bradford	$5.95
☐	27197	**CIRCLES** Doris Mortman	$5.95

Audio

☐ **SEPTEMBER** by Rosamunde Pilcher
Performance by Lynn Redgrave
180 Mins. Double Cassette   45241-X $15.95

☐ **THE SHELL SEEKERS** by Rosamunde Pilcher
Performance by Lynn Redgrave
180 Mins. Double Cassette   48183-9 $14.95

☐ **THE EVENING NEWS** by Arthur Hailey
Performance by Fritz Weaver
180 Mins. Double Cassette   45223-1 $14.95

☐ **COLD SASSY TREE** by Olive Ann Burns
Performance by Richard Thomas
180 Mins. Double Cassette   45166-9 $14.95
